# EUROPE
## IN WOMEN'S SHORT STORIES FROM TURKEY

Edited by Gültekin Emre

**Milet Publishing**
Smallfields Cottage, Cox Green
Rudgwick, Horsham, West Sussex
RH12 3DE England
info@milet.com
www.milet.com
www.milet.co.uk


First English edition published by Milet Publishing in 2012

Copyright © Milet Publishing, 2012

ISBN 978 1 84059 767 7

First published in Turkish as *Kadın Öykülerinde Avrupa* in 2010

With thanks to the Cunda International Workshop for Translators of
Turkish Literature (CWTTL/TEÇCA) for bringing together the
translators and thus launching this collaboration

Funded by the Turkish Ministry of Culture and Tourism TEDA Project

Printed and bound in Turkey by Ertem Matbaası

# Contents

## From Foreword to Turkish Edition

For many in Turkey, the streets of Europe seemed paved with gold in the 1960s and 70s, and it was often women who were left behind as men migrated there in search of work. Those days were marked by separation, grief, and hope. Then, families were reunited as their wives joined the men abroad, and children were born there, to be raised learning another language. Years later, some families returned to their towns of origin. Also, increasing numbers of Turkish nationals began visiting Europe as tourists, bringing home photographs, descriptions and memories. A body of art and literature grew that examined these patterns of life and travel abroad, as well as the meaning of citizenship. The stories in this collection, however, are not just representative of migration. Populated mainly by women protagonists, these striking narratives explore their experiences of the spaces of Europe, such as its streets, trains and airports. Speaking of melancholy and longing, but also of discovery and redemption, the stories open windows into the vibrant worlds of these women.

—Gültekin Emre
*Translated by Mark David Wyers*

## Foreword to English Edition

When the translations of the stories in this collection started rolling in, I was struck by just how different they were from the stories in *Istanbul in Women's Short Stories*, the first anthology in this series, which I co-edited. The Turkish women in *Istanbul* are on their home turf; they are center stage, in command of their surroundings and often enamored with them too. In contrast, the women of *Europe in Women's Short Stories* are a little off-center and sometimes uncertain about their terrain. Whether they are rooted in Europe or just passing through, there is always a sort of tug on them, this way or that—towards new ways or old ways, towards greater freedom or a sense of security. They're pulled outward and inward; in the encounter with Europe, some characters reach out, and some retract. As their identities are tested by difference or shift into flux, the women take risks and let their hair down in ways they might not do so easily in Turkey. But even in Europe, it's never that simple; they can face resistance—in the host cultures, in their families, in themselves...

This experience of difference and flux generates diverse forms of writing, and not all serious. The collection is dotted with light-hearted, chatty, chick lit-type stories that were unexpected for me, and pleasantly so. Still, I'll admit I am most compelled by the heavier works—the politicized, passionate sort of writing that I expected to find. Mine Söğüt's chilling "Death in a Merciless Country", powerfully translated by İdil Aydoğan, encapsulates a life and death between two places and achieves something enormous in four pages. "Fragile City" finds Suzan Samancı back in the turbulent eastern city of Diyarbakır, overwhelmed by the heat and flashbacks of struggle. While she's been in Stockholm, Diyarbakır has remained unchanged, and inside, she too remains the same: her life abroad has not erased her pain, nor has it diminished her hope for peace. The story is beautifully translated by Alvin Parmar, who described it as "more like an extended prose poem than a short story". Zeynep Avcı takes the form to new dimensions with her multi-narrative work, "Short Stories: Apprentices of Life Abroad", made up of five poignant tales, just a page each—brilliant, and brilliantly translated by Mark David Wyers.

The Europe of the title is broken down into parts in the stories. Many of them take place in Germany, especially in Berlin, but this opens up for us multiple Berlins—what Karin Karakaşlı aptly describes as a "Matryoshka of Cities", like Istanbul. We are brought to Britain, France, the Netherlands and other northern climes, and in "The Dark Call of Water" by Erendiz Atasü, we're taken to a heady Venice. Inevitably, some of the Turkish characters face prejudice in Europe—or they fear it, as vividly depicted in "Delusions in the Heart of a Giant" by Yasemin Yazıcı. Sometimes they bring their own prejudices with them; a few out of step, essentialist comments on race needed finessing in editing. While there are misunderstandings in the Turkish–European encounters in these pages, there are also many understandings; boundaries are genuinely crossed.

The contributors to this collection range from established to emerging authors, and two are no longer with us. Many of the stories were written in 2010 for the Turkish edition, some in the 1980s and 1990s, and one in 1975. The writers represent different generations and different ethnic backgrounds in Turkey, but they have in common a journey to Europe—as a refugee, an immigrant, a conference participant, a student, an au pair, a tourist… For a simple or life-or-death reason, they each take a leap. Most of them land; some stay and make Europe their home. Many remain liminal, existing in the proverbial in-between—a precarious position but one that allows dual perspectives. Those views are woven into the stories with acuity and generosity, at times with anger, but also with love. These writers and their characters find ways out; they look for ways in, and ways back. More than anything, they strive to find, to construct ways to *be*—as travelers, immigrants, as people who take leaps—wherever they may be.

—Patricia Billings

## Editorial Notes

Throughout the stories in this collection, we have retained the Turkish for several types of terms, including personal names, honorifics, place names and foods, among others. We have used the English spelling of Istanbul, rather than its Turkish spelling, İstanbul, because the English version is so commonly known. For the Turkish terms and other foreign language terms, we have used italics in their first instance in each story and then normal text for subsequent instances in the same story.

The translators represented here write primarily in British English or American English. In this edition, we have aimed for a "mid-Atlantic" pitch, using terms and idioms from both dialects, but mainly US spellings. For stories set in Britain, we have retained the British dialect.

## Guide to Turkish Pronunciation

Turkish letters that appear in the stories and which may be unfamiliar are shown below, with a guide to their pronunciation.

c    as *j* in 'just'
ç    as *ch* in 'child'
ğ    silent, but lengthens the preceding vowel
ı    as *a* in 'along'
ö    as German *ö* in 'Köln', or French *oe* in 'oeuf'
ş    as *sh* in 'ship'
ü    as German *ü* in 'fünf', or French *u* in 'tu'
ˆ    accent over vowel: syllable is stressed, as *â* in 'Leylâ'

# Frau Adler and the Berlin Train

Buket Uzuner

*Translated by Mark David Wyers*

If I hadn't been on the Berlin train that day, I never would have met Frau Adler. I would not have heard one of the world's most touching love stories, the story of a sixty-five year old woman in the midst of a passionate romance. Not until she was on another journey and told her tale to another writer, and not until it was written and published, and I came across it. Among the best things in life are these small stories that bear so much hope.

"Excuse me, dear, I am on a trip that will last one hour and twenty-one minutes. However, when the train arrives at the Hildesheim station, I just must be sitting in the window seat. I hope that will not be a problem, my dear?"

It is a miracle to hear a German speaking English in the heart of Germany, and I looked up to see who was addressing me. The speaker was an elderly woman with blue eyes that sparkled with the glint of life. She was wearing a navy coat and blue sweater set, and a large brown purse was slung over her arm. Something about her was striking, but her attractiveness was somehow timeless, giving you the impression that she was of another era. Perhaps that is what drew me to her? On this trip, I had found myself sitting next to the window for the first time in years. As I was thinking about how to answer her question, she hung her coat on the hook, settled into the aisle seat, and continued talking in the most intimate terms, as if we were close friends who had last seen each other not long before. She stopped speaking for a moment and signaled with her hands that I was still wearing my headphones.

Leaning towards me, she whispered, "Ah, my dear, when I saw that you were listening to a Virginia Woolf novel, I thought you were English. Unfortunately, we Germans do not often read Woolf." She gave a quick, sweet laugh, and the train pulled out from the Fulda station.

My trip from Frankfurt to Berlin was the idea of my Turkish–German friends who wanted to make a present of the journey, as they knew of my fondness for train travel. Turkish–Germans have become so accustomed to the speed, safety and comfort of train travel in Europe that perhaps they find it strange that someone like me who spends half the year traveling around Turkey would still prefer flying over taking the train. But European trains are exotic to me. Turkish trains, in every regard, are relics from the 1930s: slow and rickety, they are rolling museums of the past stuck in the days of the folk song "Ley ley limi limi ley". It is not because the successive governments in Turkey didn't like trains; they were just far more interested in constructing roads and in the petroleum industry. Turkey long held the record in Europe for the highest price of gasoline, for road travel, and for traffic accidents. It is still that way.

I had participated in some bilingual Turkish and German literary events held in various cities around Germany, and before this two-week tour was finished and I headed back to Istanbul, the last stop on my itinerary was Berlin. This was my first time visiting the city. It seemed to me that if you hadn't been to Berlin, you just hadn't been to Europe, and I was excited to see the city in a way that only city lovers can feel. For my trip, I had been seen off at the grandiose and ultra-modern Frankfurt Main Hauptbanhof by eight bilingual, third generation Turkish–Germans who had succeeded well in their professional lives. According to my calculations, the length of the journey was 560 kilometers, and by taking into account the ten stops, which would add thirty minutes to the trip, it would take four hours and six minutes on the modern double-decker train traveling at 160 kilometers per hour. I approached the train, admiring yet again the technology and human effort that could transform metal into such a beautiful and practical work of art. The train was white embellished with a red stripe, and the long front, which tapered like a nose, sloped down to the tracks, and with its two side windows, it resembled a passenger-carrying snake with slanted, clever eyes.

As a rule I always sit in the aisle seat when I travel, but this time I wanted to sit by the window so that I could take in the lush views of the German countryside. Having placed my bag on the overhead shelf at the very front of the train car, I hung my coat on the hook and settled into the wide, comfortable seat. I put my water bottle and travel journal in the seat-back pocket, and inserted into my Walkman the tape of Virginia Woolf's *A Room of One's Own* that I had bought from a shop in Frankfurt that sold English-language books. In those years, it wasn't common to find audio recordings of books on CD; they were still just on tape. I pressed play on my Walkman and began listening with pleasure to a Shakespearean actor reading the novel. The seat next to me was empty. The train began moving, and I waved to my Turkish–German hosts on the platform; even though they were third generation, they still maintained that Turkish tradition of waiting and waving when your train departed, a tradition that will surely die out in the near future as the pace of life continues to quicken and people lack the time for such graces. The further we traveled from Frankfurt, the more beautiful the scenery became with its German greenness and carefully tended fields, and I gave myself over to Virginia Woolf's novel. This is how the trip from Frankfurt to Fulda passed, except for brief stops as passengers got on and off the train, until Frau Adler boarded. Our paths crossed, on the premise that I was the only passenger with an audio tape of Virginia Woolf; and, like most people who have a good story, she launched straight into hers. Before continuing, however, I should point out that I told her that I was not English. I felt this was necessary because, as a result of the Turkish laborers who went to Germany in the 1960s and then settled there, German thinking about Turks has remained inflected, and both cultures have suffered as a result of the culture shock that has ensued. For this reason, it is more difficult to be a Turk in Germany than any other nationality. In all honesty, I was afraid that if I told Frau Adler that I was Turkish, she might not tell me her story. Everything indicated that the story was a good one, and in fact, for travelers and writers, the best travel gift you can ever receive is a good story. I only had a few seconds to decide whether or not to run the risk. In the end, I opted to be honest with her, and told her I wasn't English.

"Oh really, dear," she said, "I didn't really think you looked English anyways, because I know the English very well. After the war, I went to England to study. But of course, my dear, in those days I was quite young and attractive." She adjusted her short hair, which was dyed blond to cover the gray. It seemed that she wasn't interested in where I was from, or just didn't care; either she was a humanist who thought in universal terms or was so selfish that she had to always be the center of attention.

"Of course, after the war, being German wasn't easy, especially in England, but you know, the English are such polite people," she sighed. She shook her head, and it was as though she had read my thoughts, which for a fleeting moment made me feel uneasy.

"My name is Adler, Frau Adler," she smiled, seemingly to have completely forgotten the unpleasant topic we had just been discussing. At that point it was my turn to introduce myself, but without a hitch, she continued: "In English, my dear, Adler means 'eagle'. But is there anything about me that resembles an eagle?" she said, and laughed. She may have been even older than sixty-five, but there was something so feminine about her that indeed the surname "eagle" did not suit her. At best, it could have been "pigeon" or "turtledove".

"My dearly departed husband's surname was Adler. I was married long enough to have forgotten my maiden name! But of course you, my dear, are too young to know what such a long marriage means. But it would be unfair for me to complain, because my husband was a very good man. I can't recall a single incident when he was rude or hurtful, and as far as I know, not once did he ever cheat on me. He was a well-intentioned and polite man. But he had absolutely no interest in litera-ture or the arts, nor did he have a hobby or any other interests. Since I had studied to be a secretary in England and spoke English, I had the chance to work with top-level managers, which meant that I had had the opportunity to marry such men. That's a tradition, you know, aging managers like to marry young secretaries! But those men with their flashy diplomas feel so free to flirt with the secretaries while their wives are at home, and this means that after a few years, they would do the same to us, don't you agree? Keeping this in mind, I turned down all of the marriage proposals I received. Well of course, my dear, there were only two," she said, and this time I laughed with her, because her sense of humor was much like my own.

"The company where I worked dealt in office equipment like pens, paper, folders and card indexes. In those days, our products had the largest market share. Of course, there weren't any kinds of electronic correspondence in those days, I am talking about the 1950s! Anyways, in the accounting department of the company there was a handsome but shy man by the name of Adler, and like me, his salary was quite small. But I guessed that he would make a better husband than any of those old pot-bellied managers, and one day during the lunch break I invited him to have a beer. Bashfully, he accepted. We began dating, and then we got married. Ah, my dear, we even had a daughter," she said, and as she said this, her voice trembled and broke. I sensed that it would be inappropriate to ask more, and trusting my instincts, I remained silent.

"Now you are going to ask me," she said, the cheer returning to Frau Adler's voice, "what happened to the manager of the company?" I said nothing, and in any case, she was making it clear which questions I needed to ask. "The following year, Herr Direktor moved out, left his wife and children, and married a young secretary who worked at the company. You know, my dear, that once a man sets his mind on being with a new woman, her personality matters not a whit. Old men just don't have much time left! It has always been this way, but thank God there are always exceptions. Helmut is one of those…"

At that moment the train stopped at a station, but I no longer had any interest whatsoever in learning the name of the station, listening to Virginia Woolf or making notes in my travel journal. I was so enchanted that I had put everything out of my mind except hearing the story to the end before the one hour and twenty-one minute journey was over, and we had already covered much of the distance. I had even ceased thinking about my impending visit to Berlin, and about Karl who would be waiting for me at the station with a red carnation.

"Helmut was the husband of my childhood friend Heike. In those days, we Adlers would visit them as a family... That's life. If we knew what was going to happen to us, perhaps we would lose our love for living. One day you will forget me and the friendship we found on this train, but remember this: no matter what happens, we should always keep hope, because so long as you have hope, you can still live, my dear."

As the train got underway again, I felt confused. It was clear that Helmut, the "exception", was not her departed Herr Adler, and what's more, he was her friend's husband. The scent of coffee drifted into the train car, and I took a deep breath, as this was my way of saving myself whenever I began to feel irritated. Rather than asking about Helmut, I blurted, "Frau Adler, could I invite you to the dining car for a cup of coffee?" She replied, "No, no, that is just not possible, I never budge from my seat until I arrive in Hildesheim, and when we get there I just must sit by the window because as we pull into the station, Helmut must see me waving to him from the window. This is how it always happens." It occurred to me that waving at the station had also been a tradition in Germany at some time in the past. It also struck me that Frau Adler could be a complete lunatic and that, after her husband's death, she made up this Helmut character and was just entertaining herself in her remaining days by finding foreigners on trains and pitching them her stories. I felt annoyed. Everything changes when you begin to suspect that someone you were taking seriously might just be crazy. That suspicion sets up a rift and begins to poison the relationship. As I was thinking this (perhaps she had even made up her name?), Frau

Adler reached down to her imitation brown purse which was on the floor in front of her seat. Placing the purse on her knees, she removed a small thermos. The thermos was of the old type, and it reminded me of how, when I was a child and we went on picnics with my parents, my mother would open the thermos and swell with pride, "It is still hot!" and offer us tea; to refuse that tea was just about a sin. The coffee that Frau Adler offered me was truly exquisite and steaming hot as well. And as if that weren't enough, she reached into her purse and offered me two squares of bitter chocolate. I wanted to say something in return for her kindness, but again she spoke first, "Bitter coffee goes so well with bitter chocolate. My dear Herr Adler also liked it very much…" Now you're going too far; you steal your best friend's husband, and then bereave your husband while eating chocolate. That takes the cake! I realized that I had quickly brought myself to a dead end with this situation and didn't want to talk anymore. I fell silent. Moreover, I had begun to dislike Frau Adler's story to the point that I wondered if she was mischievously spinning some literary tale about a life that could actually be summed up in a minute. Indeed, she might have been crazy, but there was a chance that her convoluted way of moving through the narration and her creativity were intended to pull in the listener. Didn't this possibility alone show that she was a rather clever and unique individual? Perhaps occasionally she boards a train and, catching the eye of a foreigner, tells this story and by thoroughly confusing her listener sets off on her own personal adventure? Maybe next time she tells the story, I will be in it as well?

"But people can't live out their lives in mourning. Our youth was consumed by the war and its destruction. It was darkened by poverty, guilt, defeat and alienation. We lost our loved ones. We suffered so many losses, so many. And then we looked around and saw that we had grown old. If you don't believe in reincarnation, you must seize what is left of your life with all your heart and enjoy what happiness you can find. Isn't that so, my dear?"

By that point, my initial enthusiasm had faded, but having accepted being part of the game, I agreed. But I also wanted to surprise her, and to be honest, to frighten her a little. Without skipping a beat, I said in a soft voice, "I am a writer. A novelist, a writer of fiction." But Frau Adler was not taken aback. It seemed that it would make no difference to her if she were telling her story to a writer, a chemist or an astronaut. "Oh, I am so pleased to meet you," she said flatly. "I had actually guessed that you might be a writer by the way that you so carefully observe your surroundings and your intimate way of listening to my story. I was saying to myself, this lady might be a reporter or an academic, and look, I was right! Aside from attending book signings and being a member of a reading group, I have never had the chance to meet a writer. As I mentioned before, Herr Adler had no interest in the arts, and in order not to hurt him, I always held myself back and behaved prudently, my dear."

She looked at her watch and paused. "I am going to the ladies room to freshen my makeup, but I am going to leave my coat here. You will be here, won't you?" she said and quickly got up. I have heard restrooms referred to many ways, but this 1950s way of saying "ladies room" with her British English accent was very Frau Adler. She had left nothing behind that I could scrutinize, no clues about her identity. Her coat was hanging there, but as much as I wanted to check the pockets, I couldn't bring myself to do it. In any case, she quickly returned, her cheeks rouged rose and her thin lips glistening light pink, and she had put on lilac-scented perfume.

"It would be best if I sat in the window seat now, as we will be arriving in Hildesheim in about twenty minutes," she said, as though we had already agreed on the seating arrangement. I did the only thing possible and moved over to the aisle seat. When she sat down, Frau Adler wiped the window clean with a tissue she brought with her, and then she wrung her hands anxiously. She leaned down and got a tube of hand cream from her purse, then rubbed the cream into her hands. By now her excitement was tangible. Perhaps there was really somebody named Helmut waiting for her at the station? And if so, was he really her friend's husband? If this was true, what kind of man was this Helmut, and at this age, how could he excite a woman so much?

Suddenly she said, "Both of our spouses had passed way." It was as if this were part of the game: she would notice I was sitting chin in palm, lost in thought, and then tell me this. So I didn't respond. She ignored my silence: "Herr Adler suffered through a long and difficult struggle with cancer. I looked after him for a full five years. Looking after someone who is ill, especially someone you love, is a heartrending experience. In the final stages, he was suffering so much that sometimes I had to run to the kitchen and weep in secret. At times something inside me rebelled against the fact that a person could suffer so terribly, and I wanted to save him from that pain. I considered euthanasia, but couldn't go through with it. Rather, I enrolled in a nursing course so that I could better look after him and make sure that his death would be as *comfortable* as possible. I cannot explain how difficult it is to watch someone die, someone you have shared so many years with, a close friend, someone with whom you found a special language for life. May God never make you suffer that, my dear," she said and with a deft gesture wiped away her tears with her pinkie.

"When he died, I was left utterly alone, utterly! As if everyone in the world counted except for me. Aside from Herr Adler, I knew no

one, and when he passed away, I had become invisible. I also wanted
to die to save myself. A few times I even tried, but dying is not so easy.
Before Herr Adler passed on, I had retired, and since I had nothing to
do, being at home alone was torture," she said and fell silent. Then, as
though we had never met, she turned and began watching the scenery
passing by outside the window. At that moment, I remembered that we
weren't alone on the train. Turning slightly, I peered around the train
car. On the other side of the aisle across from me a young German
was reading a book, an elderly couple was dozing in the seats behind
us, and across from them a businessman was reading a newspaper. Not
knowing what to do, I turned forward and gazed at Frau Adler from
the corner of my eye. Her thick skin-colored stockings completely concealed the skin beneath. Her dark blue shoes were new, but the cloth of
her matching blue skirt, which extended below her knees, was slightly
worn. Her elegant, blue-veined hands, which she was rubbing in her
lap, were covered in age spots.

"I was despondent. All of my hope and enthusiasm had abandoned
me. That's when I fell into depression," she said, without turning to look
at me, and again surreptitiously wiped away her tears with her pinkie.
I wanted to ask what had happened to her daughter, but because of her
weeping, I held back. "For a while I volunteered in the children's ward
of the hospital, but that saddened me even more." Again the pinkie
maneuver.

The train stopped, but not at a station. Perhaps we were waiting
for a train to pass or they were switching the tracks. "Ah, we are so
near!" Frau Adler sighed. Then turning to me and closing her eyes, she
asked, "Has my makeup run?" I looked at her. First I saw the wrinkles
beneath the foundation and powder. Then I saw the traces of suffering
and the melancholy that she tried to conceal with the cheer in voice. In

the white skin of the face she held out for me as if it were an offering, I also saw the cruel lines of a life of 65 or 70 years in which she had found no respite. Her frail face floated before me like a cross-section of human life, fragile and mortal, greedy and arrogant. I thought to myself, if someone offers their face for you to examine, you have to believe them. In a gentle tone of voice, I said, "A little lipstick would be good." She opened her purse, fished out a plastic mirror, and carefully applied the lipstick. She looked at me as if to say, "Is this okay?" Smiling, I nodded.

"Helmut's wife Heike, my old friend, also came down with cancer, but she passed quickly without suffering too much. That pleases people, you know? Anyways, after all of this pain and loss, one day I took myself to a Liszt concert. I say 'took' because in those days it was like I had a split personality and was living with two Frau Adlers. The Frau Adler who wanted to live had to carry around the Frau Adler that wanted to die. It was there at the concert, three years ago, that I ran into Helmut; I will never forget it. It was a spring concert at the baroque Fulda Cathedral. That's where I saw him. I was so happy that I wanted to run over and throw my arms around him. Helmut was someone from my past and it felt like he was the only person I knew in the world. But Heike, like Herr Adler, also didn't like to go out much. That's why, when they lived in Fulda, we only made home visits. That day when I saw Helmut and asked about Heike, that big man broke down in tears in front of everyone at the concert. I noticed that when I told him Herr Adler had passed away, it was the first time I had accepted his death. Isn't that strange? After that, we never parted again!" I tried to imagine them as two elderly people in a concert hall trying to console each other. But since my bank of images was stocked by Hollywood and Turkish films, I struggled to find a reference for two elderly people in love because in all of those films, the lovers are either both young, or an older man with a younger woman.

"I will never forget, we asked a lot of people to change seats so that we could sit next to each other, but nobody would, so after the German pianist—I can't remember his name now, how forgetful I have become!—started playing Chopin's "Heroic" Polonaise, we nearly broke our necks trying to look at each other! Can you imagine it, two old widows gazing at each other like young lovers. It was splendid, just splendid! But it would be a lie if I said that it was easy at at first. Both of our spouses had passed away, and we had fallen in love with each other. It is a shameful state of affairs. In the beginning, when we held hands we were embarrassed, as though Herr Adler and Heike could see us and were reprimanding us. And when we kissed, it felt like they were watching us, not to mention when we were in bed together! Don't ask about that, my dear. But of course, you haven't seen him; Helmut is an unbelievably handsome, extremely dashing, charming and sexy man!" she said, and as though she were describing a delectable recipe, she smacked her lips. I was bewildered, my head reeled. While I could recall having felt that drunken enthusiasm with which she described Helmut, particularly in that last part, I suddenly realized with a clench in my heart that although I may have been the age of Frau Adler's daughter, I had not described a man with such passion in a very long time.

"There is something I would like to ask of you. When we arrive in Hildesheim, I am going to disembark from the train, and just like every week, I am going to hug Helmut and he is going to kiss me. Then I will place my arm in his and lean against his strong shoulder. At that moment I will turn and look at you, and if you like him, I would like you to raise your index finger. If you don't like him, raise two fingers, like the 'victory' sign, okay? But you must be honest with me, no tricks. If you like him, one finger, if you dislike him two fingers, do you promise?" I opened my mouth as if to say, "This is too much!" but I could see that she was seriously waiting for me to promise. I began laughing. It was infectious and she began giggling too. We laughed until our sides ached, in a celebration of laughter as the most wonderful gift bestowed upon humanity. It felt so good, and when we noticed this, we laughed even more. When she quieted down, she asked me again: "Do you promise?" "Yes!" I replied, still laughing. Just then I heard the word "Hildesheim" in the German announcement made over the loudspeaker. This meant that soon I would be parted from Frau Adler. I hadn't thought I would be upset about this, but it seemed I would. Her excitement was plain to see when the announcement came, and I couldn't bear it any longer: "You have been meeting in train stations for three years. Why don't you just move in together?" I asked. The creases of laughter still visible in her face, she gazed out the window as we pulled into the city. "It is more romantic this way," she replied. "One week he comes to me, and the other week I go to him. But every time we meet, it is so nostalgic and romantic, like in the old movies." She turned and caught me scowling. "Also, I need my husband's retirement fund, and if I marry, I will lose it," she whispered. It was plain to see that she understood I didn't like what she had said: "My dear writer, I am a fiercely independent woman. If we lived together, do you think that Helmut would get dressed up like that to meet me at the station twice a month, or that I would be so excited to see him? Don't you know, my dear, that living together kills the passion?"

The train slowed and pulled into the station. Frau Adler's spirit had soared in excitement, leaving behind her tall bony frame. The train stopped. She sighed, "There he is!" Then I saw him waving as he approached the window, a tall flat-bellied youthful-looking man wearing a brown suede coat, his white hair slicked back. His dazzling white teeth shone (were they porcelain?) as he smiled at her with a rakish grin. She leapt up with the litheness of a young woman and gathered up her coat and purse. I stood up to let her out, and she hugged me tightly, kissing me on the cheek. "If you would like, one day you can write my story. But in any case, my dear, you don't know my real name!" she said. I silently followed her all the way to the stairs. As she descended, without turning back she said, "I had always wanted to go to Istanbul!" I heard myself reply in Turkish, "Enough already!" In a daze, I returned to my window seat, from where I saw that Frau Adler was arm in arm with Helmut, her back to me as they headed towards the exit. Their still spry bodies were pressed against each other as they walked, their steps in stride, the body language of people in love. When the train began to pull out for Berlin, Frau Adler turned slightly and looked at me. I raised my index finger, and when she saw this, she smiled with pleasure. I waved with my finger still raised, like a student asking to be excused from the classroom, and they both stopped and waved back. I didn't know this couple one hour and twenty-one minutes ago, and now they were now waving me off from Hildesheim to Berlin like old friends. If anyone else told me this, I wouldn't believe them, but as those two people who I would never see again disappeared in the crowd of the station, my heart was stricken by a heaviness. I smiled wryly as I picked up my Walkman so that I could continue from where I left off, and just then I noticed that "Made in Turkey" was printed on the tag of my coat. This time my smile was genuine: there was no sadness at all. No matter what her real name was, no matter how her husband and daughter had passed away, Frau Adler truly believed during that train journey that I would write her story. Sooner or later I would, because among the best things in life are those small stories that bear so much hope.

When I got off the train in Berlin, I was met by Karl, who told me that on my cheek there was a smudge of pink lipstick.

# Matryoshka of Cities

Karin Karakaşlı

*Translated by Mark David Wyers*

Berlin
Istanbul
Berlin
Istanbul

It was a day that took after the paintings of Chagall; I floated in the air, along with all of the pieces of my past; after all, love is a state of being that knows nothing of the rules of gravity. As I floated in the air, these old life pieces, which would not mean anything to anyone else at first glance, fluttered around me: a maritime ferry, a well-worn cobblestone slope, the baptistery in the church where I was baptized, the frosted pane of glass of which I insisted on kissing, a large wall clock in who knows which house that chimes every fifteen minutes, the choppy Black Sea coastline of the gray-green Bosphorus, a *simit* seller hawking bread rings and yogurt ayran drink, a street flower vendor with her daisies and jonquils.

Actually, I just wanted to gather up myself and go, but that thing called "myself" is composed of such details. When trying to describe yourself, they never come to mind, but when you try to stitch together sentences defining who you are, it is always those small details that you recall, one after another. They follow you, without becoming a burden or an annoyance.

Without becoming a burden or an annoyance, I followed him… Out of love. I alighted in Berlin, because he was there, and when you love someone, you don't go to a city, you arrive there. But if that person isn't there waiting, only the city greets you. Berlin opens its arms.

Still, all I wanted was to go to him. In that city upon which the first rays of dawn fall, to float down to him, to be his dream. But the morning light was so intense and gray that I paused in the city square. Such a harsh light can make you weary of life. Like in all northern cities, waking up in Berlin is hard work. That's why the inhabitants of some places, including Berlin, should be thought of as doing double shifts in the eyes of God.

Those who had to awaken, as well as those who had nothing to do, had long gotten up. The city belonged to students, to tourists, and along with early-rising officials, to the workers. Those early wakers can only find their way if their destinations are programmed into their automatic pilots. If you are not one of them and you find yourself on the streets at that early hour, it means that, like me, you didn't have a place inside. Because of your impatient excitement…

The time of my impatience is that early hour before cafes and shops open. The square in which I alighted, near the Brandenburg Gate, is home to the Holocaust Memorial, home to a testimony that has nothing to do with working hours. Hitler's bombed-out military headquarters are a few hundred meters to the south, and the bunker is under the parking lot. There are 2,711 concrete blocks in the monument. You can describe it that way: a few figures, a few geographical coordinates, and two dry historical details. But that doesn't explain it. Just like that uncanny feeling of translation when you try describing love to a third person, it just can't be explained.

I am at the center of the concrete blocks. Thousands of concrete blocks. They trace the line of the horizon. Some of the cold gray columns are horizontal, and some are vertical. The ground is sloped and undulates. The optical illusion calls to mind the myriad views of a shifting landscape. There are no words or inscriptions to guide these associations. It is just you and the blocks. Children are playing hide-and-seek among the columns. An elderly woman admonishes the children: "Show a little respect. This is the Holocaust Memorial." The sharpness in her voice makes the children pause for a moment, but the appeal of the place for playing hide-and-seek is overwhelming. Not long after, once again the sound of the children's shouts and laughter can be heard ringing among the columns.

The perimeter of the square and the spaces between the blocks are filled with the spirits of the dead. The spirits emerge, shimmering in their youth. There are women in fur coats, skirt suits and broad-brimmed hats, and men wearing long coats. Dining tables laden with food and handwritten letters float in the air. The spirits smile at the children. They possess understanding and care nothing for outer forms. For these spirits, not separating death and cruelty from life and hope has its good sides. Some of the more mischievous spirits silently show the children the best places to hide.

At places, it seems obvious that they are gravestones, but when you walk among them, they can be transformed into two rows of soldiers. Sometimes they rise above you and take your breath away, and then break off into an openness. Remembering should be something like this: in the circle of time, a focus on the past that is always present and also includes the future. Those spirits exist within the life of the city, among us. They are the nameless, the undescribed, all of us, and none of us. Among those blocks, a person can start their own story, and turn their own circle of time around the center as if watching someone else.

Berlin has developed a new breed of memory from its cycles of repeated destruction and rebirth. And the city's memory is the necessary cornerstone for your own small story. It's as though you cannot begin your existence until you accept that. As I walked on the sidewalks of Scheunenviertel, I saw that, between some of the paving stones, there were brass plaques bearing names: these are the names of people who once lived in those houses and were later sent to the concentration camps, the old residents of Berlin. Like a secret agreement between those names and life. A spiritual oath that changes the steps you take.

"You wait here, I want to walk around a little," I tell my life pieces. I leave behind the ferry, baptistery, cobblestone slope, coastline, wall clock, flower seller and simit seller, and begin to walk. Beneath my feet are yellowed chestnut and linden leaves. The weather is cold, but I run with a lightness and simple joy. There is a contract between myself and life never to forget and to do things differently. My feet spring from the leaves with a rustling. I could walk like this forever, because Berlin is a city that can bring you to the very ends of yourself. If you are willing to take the risk.

If you do take that risk, Berlin becomes ineluctable, but this is an ineluctability that cannot be explained to people who don't sense it, because this city is not particularly beautiful. You cannot compare it with the gondolas of Venice, the painters of Paris, or the splendor of Rome. To be loved, Berlin demands effort, but nonchalantly. You wouldn't think that a city which has been reduced to rubble so many times would beg for compassion. But sometimes those that want the least, in fact need the most. Once you have felt the pulse of the city, once you have taken hold of its windy hair, it curls up in your lap and falls into repose.

In truth, I fell in love with Berlin. But if anyone asked, I wouldn't be able to say why. A city is not something that can justify love. There are moments, meanings that you grasp. This city speaks to me of an indivisible, cyclical time. It appears before me, with all of its proud women. Hundreds of women stand timeless before the detention center on Rosenstrasse where their husbands were held en route to Auschwitz. So long as it remains in memory, this is not a painting that was frozen in the winter of 1943, but rather the eternal testimony of their incalculable courage. "Gebt uns unsere Männer zurück!" the German women cried. When the police trained the barrels of their guns on the women, they shouted even louder: "Give us back our men!" The Jewish husbands were not sent to the camp. In the midst of that empire of terror, through the shouts of those women, this street writes a history that is at once small and grandiose.

Within my back, I can sense those women from the unseen world as they accompany the sound of my heels resounding on the pavement of the empty street, and as they shout, my spine straightens. I am filled with pride in women.

When I turn onto a side street, the shouts give way to an old song. The sultry voice of Marlene Dietrich speaks to me of European cities. The beauty of the Rue Madeleine in Paris, the loveliness of touring Rome in May, the quietude of a summer evening in Vienna with a glass of wine. Then, she pauses, puts in her final word: "Though you may laugh, I am still thinking of Berlin."

*Ich hab noch einen Koffer in Berlin*
*deswegen muß ich da nächstens wieder hin*

*die Seligkeiten vergangener Zeiten*
*sie sind alle immer noch in diesem kleinen Koffer drin*

*I still have a suitcase in Berlin*
*That's why I have to go there sometime soon.*
*The joys of days gone by*
*Are all still in my little suitcase.*

I also have a Berlin suitcase. It is in my heart. It is full of wine corks, wooden tables and books. And you are in my heart, next to my suitcase. Not knowing what to do with the suitcase, you stand there, buttoning up your coat.

I button up my coat tightly. I can measure the passage of time by my frozen nose and numb fingertips. From the kiosk on the corner, I buy a bottle of mulled wine. Inhaling its scents, I drink of Berlin. I ingest it all: the workers' district of Wedding; the prim homes of Charlottenburg; the laughable yet despairing contrast between Alex with its television tower dating from the time of the Eastern Bloc and the Middle Ages air of its next-door neighbor Nikolai; Kreuzberg, the east of which has become known for its Turkish immigrants, *döner* restaurants selling grilled meat, and tea-scented notions shops, while the west basks in its swanky bohemian airs; the traces of the Prussian, Weimar and Socialist eras that fell like dominoes; the sleek, glimmering shopping centers; the open markets in the squares; the Asian transiency of Neukölln which has become home to immigrants of every nationality in the world. Berlin is all of these, and more. A teller of tales that unfolds its story, including each and every newcomer.

With a single step, I launch into the air. Straight towards the old pieces of myself. I gather them up from the square and soar to his home. There is no one there. Just the sound of my own breathing.

*It was five in the morning when the woman and man went into his house. The night was pitch-dark and cold. Pitch-black, biting chill. "Come, I'll show you the rooms," he said. Like a real estate agent on call, he showed her the rooms of his house. The rooms of his loneliness. "Look, this is where I feed the birds. They come to eat the bread crumbs I leave there every morning. These are my plants, every morning I water them." Then he pulled the woman close to him. "This is where I work. I do the handwritten work at this small table, and the computer work at the big desk." They stopped in front of the window. "That large shadow there is actually a stream, but it has frozen over." Upon saying this he stopped, and then they embraced each other tightly.*

*Months later, while they were sitting on the shore of that stream, the ice of which had recently melted, the man asked, "Have you ever been to my place before?" She wanted to snap, "Being with so many women will naturally make you forgetful." She wanted to hurl the blood, the shreds of bloody heart wounded by the arrow of his words into his broad face, which she found so beautiful. But when she opened her mouth, she could only laugh bitterly.*

*Suddenly she remembered the morning that she left his flat. By mistake she went out the door leading to the garden and the door closed behind, leaving her trapped. She tried for a long time to find another way out, but couldn't. He found her, and they laughed and embraced passionately at the threshold.*

*She looked into his eyes. "Let me remind you," she said. "I was trapped in the garden, and you saved me." The word "saved" made her laugh again, with that same bitterness. Then she leaned back in her chair and observed the impact of her words on his face. "I remember," he said, blushing slightly. She said to herself, "Nice work, you bastard." She gulped down her cold coffee and over that voice she kept silent.*

Most of the time, love is a disaster of timing.

The fold-away bed is closed. The house is shrouded in darkness except for the office, the only room getting any light. I walk towards the office. The word "Istanbul" is written above some of the dates on the desk calendar. Desperately, I try to remember today's date. The word "Istanbul" is written above today.

Suddenly you say to yourself, "He has gone to Istanbul." Your heart flutters. A moment later, you recover. Completing the sentence, you say, "He has gone to Istanbul, but not to see you." In any case, you are here because you didn't even know he was coming. Actually, life is comprised of skating across time and space. At times, you gently touch down near one another; at others, you merely graze off. But let's not talk about the collisions that bring the two of you crashing down.

When I awake, I am in my own bed. I look at the ceiling in my dark room. Just a while ago there was a hole in the ceiling; from that hole emerged the ferry, simit seller, flower seller, coastline, wall clock, steep cobblestone street, and the baptistery, and I was flying with them in the sky. Then the hole through which I flew closed and once again became a cracked ceiling painted in white. At that moment, I felt a weight pressing on my heart. The eagle of Prometheus descended to devour the pieces of flesh it had pecked out. Somebody should point out the limitations of these mythological archetypes. They shouldn't just appear in everyone's life and pointlessly remind us, "You are not so special or anything new. Look at this story from a thousand years ago." It is a good antidote for inflated egos, but, in my defenseless morning state, this realization wouldn't let go. Sometimes, a strength can come from within that pain, or I land a blow on the head of that eagle. Perplexed by the unexpected punch it receives, the animal retreats. I gathered up what was left of myself, and laid back down on my stomach. I was in no state to dream of my loved one; I was just cold. I hid myself under the blankets.

After warming up a little, I got up and noticed that there was a message on my phone: "Are you in Istanbul?" I looked at the lines of the parquet floor. In those lines, I saw what would happen when I said, "Yes."

Even though I knew he hadn't come for me, I got ready in a flurry of excitement, because love is foolish, it's surly and stubborn, just like the weeds that grow in the spaces between the stones of that steep cobbled road that follows me. No matter how hard you try, you can't make them grow; but, whenever they want, they can bring themselves into being. Just like love.

Then there is sunlight, light in my eyes, there is wind on the ferry, my hair blowing in the wind, and my small, warm palms. There is a light in my eyes that glints in glass and mirrors. A glimmer that even I cannot look at.

Later, I sit across from him, hopeful, even though I know he didn't come for me, because I love myself in love, this woman who opens her heart fully and without restraint. He says, "I have always lived this city through the admiring eyes of my lovers. But now, I have lost that magic." He also has words to describe himself, and a life without me, and I watch from the threshold because the fortieth door is closed to him, but I don't know about the door behind that one. He is angry because I come and go, pressing against that door, but I feel his anger only as an underwater current; our rhetoric is refined and reposed. No matter what the case, we are modern and civilized, worldly city people. Perhaps the most real thing we share is anger. At the bottom, in the depths. "I am making evening concert plans," he says, and we even buy his tickets together. If he doesn't say, "Let's enjoy some music together," what would be the point of insisting? If Berlin smiles with pity, then Istanbul leers at my ridiculous state. As I am stricken by another impossibility that I don't want to acknowledge, there is yet another life scenario at work. "Dear, I don't think I got my point across," the director says. "If he wants you, he will take you in, and the opposite is true as well; in order to take you in, he has to open up. But you know he won't."

They give children the right to ask "why". I can't ask questions, and there is no answer that could stop that eagle from tearing at my heart. What's more, I couldn't explain the eagle, since it wouldn't matter to him. He is focused on his own eagles.

Are you in Istanbul? I am in Istanbul, and the world is drenched in blood. I had bought a gift, but I couldn't give it to him. This happens with death, too. You lose your loved ones and suddenly the happiest days are like a ripping of flesh. You buy a gift, but you don't know what to do with it because it isn't suitable for a grave. Until you learn to give up buying them, these ownerless things pile up. You don't know what to do with them. I threw mine into the sea. Into the churning white wake of the ferry.

I was in Istanbul. At the end of my words, with a gift that I bequeathed to the sea. This is how it happens; you get the feeling that everything has been said. The person who loves becomes permeable, but when the two cannot be intertwined, when the soul cannot be penetrated, there is nothing left to be achieved with the other-new, new-other words that you have chosen. You comprehend that.

So I said. How much of this has been attained, and what kind of journey those words undertake in another person's heart is another story altogether. So I said. And sometimes, in order to be faithful to your dreams, you have to deny those aspects of reality that don't suit your life. Not seeing what you most want to see, not speaking with whom you most want to speak. Showing your love with the things that you don't do, the things that you cannot do.

I know the cruelty of cities. I know the biting wind in Berlin that, under your hat, bores into your skull like a drill. Standing agape at the shelves towering over you at the sprawling shopping centers. Like the woman working at the register who intentionally idles on the job. As though the man in the metro making the announcement for everyone to make way were shouting just at you. You think about how many times in your life you had to make way. And of course you were pushed back because you can't walk straight into a wall. Then someone walking past bumps into your shoulder. Actually, they would turn and apologize, but in the cruel life of cities, that's not how it is. When you turn in pain to look, you see the stranger continuing along as if nothing had happened. That stranger reminds you of people you think about sometimes, but you don't know where they are; a lost friend, an impossible love. Because he was a stranger, because of what he called to mind, he becomes a thread at the end of a knot. The ball within you unravels. In shock, you look at the thread of life in your hand.

I know the cruelty of cities. The mud in Istanbul that instantly sticks to your shoes. I know about exchanging looks with street dogs that have tagged ears, the illegal *gecekondu* neighborhoods built overnight in places where the city buses don't run and their chicken coops and roofs sheathed in tin, I know about the long walls surrounding housing developments for the rich, the neon signs of nightclubs, and the men at the *meyhane* who gaze into their glasses of pungent *rakı* as if into crystal balls, men with lost glances who scurry from the reality reflected back at them from the mirrors in the restaurant.

I know all of this, but still, my dream was beautiful. It was the sweetness of a piece of chocolate after the bitter taste of a reality you finally comprehend. Those who weep together share their pain, and those who laugh together heal their pain. I am always waiting for that laughter. It is open-hearted laughter that binds Berlin to Istanbul. In my dream, there are two city matryoshkas; we pull them out one by one, our Berlin and our Istanbul, from within us. The last city disappears from between our palms. Our hands are warm.

I look at my hands; my fingertips are frozen numb again. It is finished, I say at that moment, and warm my fingers in the palm of my other hand.

# The Dark Call of Water

Erendiz Atasü

*Translated by İdil Aydoğan*

The gray-green surface deepened into a dense dark murkiness filled with waste, fuel and seaweed. The seaweed awaited her, opening and closing its mouth at the surface of the water like carnivorous plants. If our story were written in the previous century, the woman wouldn't have been able to escape the dark call of the water. Who knows how many days it would have taken for her body to be found in the canal, tangled in seaweed. Whereas now she was going to get on a magnificent plane and return to that northern country she'd come from.

Like all port cities, this place too had multiple souls. It would drive you into confusion and frighten you. Venice, Istanbul, San Francisco... You couldn't say if they were beautiful or terrifying. They resembled deep waters, in a way. Their surface sometimes crystal clear, flickering with reflections; sometimes grayish and blurred.

The day she got off the plane, the city was slumbering inside gray fog. It was immersed in water. Each year it sank deeper into mud. The woman was excited; for a minute she thought she heard the groan of sinking buildings. The city sweated like a patient with fever. It was hard to breathe.

The tourists that filled the squares and churches, that took photographs at docks and on bridges, covered the city's skin like swarms of bugs blanketing the earth. In order to break free of this mobile blanket and touch the true core of the city, she needed time. It was only shortly before her departure that the woman could hear the true voice of the city; the city of canals.

This was a sigh filled with a yearning for life. It was passionate. When the woman heard it, she felt the resonance of life on her own skin.

The city lay curled up like a woman who'd lost her youth, her beauty spoiled, but her desires fresh. She was mortal. Her very own twin sister. She didn't look down from a pedestal with pride. She recognized the remorseless corrosion of the water that added mystery and beauty to her core. While she wanted to live in warm embraces, she was suffocating in fog.

The woman could feel life in the cells of her body; life that waited motionless under the dim light of northern countries.

And at that moment she saw him, the young man with the violin. His brown hair falling onto his shoulders, his brown beard hiding his face. She saw his honey eyes, and his mouth; innocent looks and lustful curves. His sorrowful face reminiscent of depictions of Jesus.

The woman was born and raised in northern countries. With the entrepreneurial skills she had adapted over there, she followed him. They went over bridges and canals, passed smaller squares. The young man saw the woman, but paid no notice. His lucid eyes were perhaps searching for what lay beneath ordinary shapes and appearances. The woman shut her eyes and imagined what the young man's body would be like; she felt the man's ribs press against her own skinny chest, his brown hairy legs wound around her own slim legs, squeezing them. She felt pain, followed by subtle pleasure inside. His young face was perfectly proportioned. Soft, sympathetic, undemanding. The woman looked at him with hungry eyes.

The young man had received the woman's message. "Poor thing," he thought, "how she's suffering." He felt compassion for her. The woman was tall and skinny with short hair. She was wearing trousers and flat shoes. The young man imagined her frail body, lost inside baggy clothes. What was it that had turned this body into a carnal cry? Question marks and dents: that's what the woman's body was made up of. There were dents carved between her forehead and nose, her nose and her chin, her eyebrows and cheekbones. Her chest was flat. Her body seemed like one long dent from her chest to her groin. Her posture was a painful question, curious why her dents were still left empty. Deprived of the shield of curves and feminine footsteps, the woman was nature's naked scream. A painful cry piercing the mist. The young man shrugged his shoulders. He couldn't answer her questions. He himself was in search of something else. If our story were written in the previous century, the man could've found what he was looking for in a monastery; or at least that would be where he'd continue his search. Whereas the young man was searching for the more hidden canals of the city, as the woman followed him like a shadow, right behind.

The three of them met at a small square in a poor area: the woman, the man, and the other woman. The other woman was young. The curls of her lush black hair fell onto her shoulders. Even under all the makeup she was wearing, her face was as perfect, innocent and bright as the depictions of Mary in the city's churches. She carried the curves and corners of her body with pride: her soft shoulders, beautiful breasts, well-shaped thighs, her slightly domed belly. The young man was trying to strike a deal with the young belle. The woman heard the young man's preference and immediately turned around to look at the square she hadn't really noticed until then. Blackened, rickety buildings, laundry drying on lines. The marvelous aesthetics of the city had suddenly vanished, just like that, at the end of an elegant bridge. The city had lifted its taffeta skirt and shown the holes in its tights. It was terribly two-faced, the Renaissance rising upon rubble, yet candidly and indecently revealing itself at such inappropriate places. The young man and the other woman had disappeared in the narrow staircase of one of the dark buildings. The woman walked down to the docks.

The man was ready to pay the price the brunette with the curls and ivory skin demanded, as long as she was willing to help. The whore in Mother Mary's image pressed the young man's face between her breasts with a professional compassion. Oh, these New Worlders! What good was personal freedom if a man didn't have command over his manhood? The woman was master of her trade. One look and she knew just what it was you needed. And this was exactly what the man needed: a faultless but temporary compassion of the flesh. She did her job like a masseur, a physiotherapist, a psychologist, a priest.

"Relax, babe," she told the young man. "Why are you tense? Take this as a treatment. Don't you go to the doctor for your physical health? Well, you come to me for your psychological health. That's all. Plain and simple. No one is going to question you tomorrow. Or expect some sort of return, other than the hourly rate. No one will even know. Relax. Believe me, it doesn't mean anything. There's no need to be afraid."

Oh yes, yes, yes, how beautifully said. It doesn't mean anything. It's a medical intervention. Yes, okay, phew, you really do understand me. Cure me, yes, oh yes … cure me and then be gone.

The woman squirmed under the young man like a snake; she rose and fell, squeezed, pushed, turned to her side, sat up, laid on her back and facedown. She used her hands, mouth, hair, her whole body like a virtuoso musician would use her instrument. She did whatever the young man wanted, before he could even ask for it.

Oh yes, it doesn't mean anything; no commitments, no responsibilities, no questions. Oh darling, thank you.

The young homosexual from the New World ejaculated on the Venetian whore like Niagara Falls.

And that's when he realized the woman's room smelled of onions. Her black hair spread out on the white sheets, the woman lay there like a nineteenth century Venus. She was so beautiful, the young man had to look away. Hastily he got dressed, paid her, and rushed out into the city streets to take photographs. He was strong enough to move heaven and earth.

As the woman stepped onto the gondola, she raised her head and looked at the gondolier holding her hand. She first noticed his muscular arms, dark and veined, like a bronze statue. The gondolier was sturdily built with a small head atop his striking body. His eyes seemed docile. A physical and spiritual calmness had completely deactivated the budding excitement in her core.

The gondolier knew how to treat lone women who came here in search of beauty and adventure. An exaggerated politeness, extreme admiration in the eyes, but never demanding…

The minute the woman set foot on the gondola of this sturdy built, small-headed gondolier, she knew she wouldn't spend the night alone. She no longer needed to make an effort. The gondolier would know exactly what to do.

The woman arrived first at the discothèque where they were to meet. In the dark interior, her tranquility started giving way to tension. "Calm down," she told herself, "it's the piercing lights and rackety rhythm, you know this from before."

She ordered a glass of wine. Sip by sip she regained her exterior calm; underneath was tension, and under that, a recurring disappointment and a longing for the unknown. The woman clutched onto her outer shell with a carefree smile.

And she saw the gondolier. He was dancing. Strange, he hadn't come near her. She shuddered; she was being rejected for the second time in a day. She took another sip of wine and went onto the dance floor. The gondolier wouldn't see her, he was dancing with others; perhaps he was doing it on purpose. A slight pain stung the woman's heart. She surrendered herself to the beat of the music and delirious, colorful lights. She had disconnected her brain; her spine was in control of both her emotions and her actions.

Feeling her body freed from her mind's control filled the woman with childish joy. Nothing mattered anymore. Not the melancholic and calm North, or the beautiful but revolting Mediterranean, the pale-faced young musician, the sturdy and small-headed gondolier. She was alive, she was herself; she was one with her primal core, with her body.

Suddenly, she came face to face with the gondolier. Her core that had been reduced to its simplest state now rose again with delicate excitement. The woman welcomed emotions; she opened her arms and touched the gondolier.

They left the discothèque together, the gondolier and the woman. And just then, what an odd coincidence, she saw him again: Jesus with the honey-colored eyes. They both stopped and looked at each other with wide eyes. Two strangers. No, two confidants, perhaps partners in crime. The woman couldn't manage to pull her body away from the command of her spine and back to her brain. She stared emptily at the New Worlder.

As for the young man, he gazed as if he was seeing extraordinary beauty for the very first time. He was radiating the energy he had caught from the Venetian whore. How meaningful were the woman's deep-set eyes. How slim and elegant she was, like fragile porcelain. One ought to touch her without hurting her, without damaging her. How could the giant next to her truly treasure her?

The gondolier was annoyed.

"Do you know him?" he asked the woman.

"No," the woman said in a cheerful tone of voice. "I've never seen him before."


The woman lay down, satisfied. She was so pleased with her physique which she found unattractive and covered up at other times, that she spread out her bony body, stark naked. She listened to the arias the gondolier was singing in the shower, trying to deepen his voice. The gondolier was one of those who thought being Italian was enough to sing opera. The woman was catching out his faults one by one, silently; the zest flowing through her body was on a steady rise. She thought that she wouldn't have been able to lie there so contentedly if she hadn't come across the young man with the dreamy eyes on the way out of the discothèque.

While making love to the gondolier, in her mind's eye she had pictured Venice, a Venice singing starry love songs in the navy blue night. The liquid between her legs was like canals sneaking into the hidden corners of Venice. She was now sure she'd visited this city, that she'd lived here. She had slept in her arms.

She had been thinking about the young man ever since she woke up.

Over and over she envisaged the young man's unrelenting gaze; and she remembered again her own wanton voice saying "I've never seen him before." She envisaged the expression on her face as she spoke these words. She must have said it with languid eyes and a hopeful mouth. She was the happiest woman in Venice.

The young man was out of spirits. God only knew how that yahoo was treating the woman with a deep gaze. You could talk to a woman like her all night long, play her the finest violin sonatas and open your whole heart to her. As for the gondolier, what could he possibly offer her? He could only batter her with his primitive strength. He felt an unbearable craving to squeeze the woman in his arms and press her mouth against his own. He had to find the woman and take her away from the gondolier. He would search the whole of Venice till dawn. What if he couldn't see her again? He set off, wandering hopelessly.

And there she was at the corner, the belle whore from this morning. The young man was startled, his feet already on their way towards the beauty with the black curls, like a child running to its mother. He hesitated. What a proud posture she had; bolt upright breasts, hair like a mane. There was no sign at all of sensitivity, fragility, or the feeling of defeat. This was nothing but an aggressive stance. The New Worlder didn't feel that his words or his actions would move the whore's emotions.

When they bumped into each other outside the discothèque, lightning had struck in the woman's large, deep-set eyes, and the young man saw what had remained in the dark, unnoticed by him, until then: to impress the woman, he would only need to utter a single word. When the sentence "I've never seen him before" was spoken, it had cut down the young man's self-esteem. But now, a couple hours later, he had figured out that the actual meaning of these words was completely different. The young man and the woman were made for each other.

The whore gave a friendly wave. The young man pushed his hair back and grabbed his violin.

"Hi," he said uncomfortably, "I'm looking for a friend of mine."

The girl laughed in a know-it-all manner.

The young man blushed.

"I don't know her name or her address. She's with a gondolier."

The whore smiled.

"You're not looking for a friend, you're looking for someone you'd like to befriend, isn't that right?"

These were the dead hours of her trade. She could help this newbie out.

"There are a couple of places where gondoliers take traveling women. We can go and take a look."


The woman walked beside the dark canal like a shadow in mourning. She had never felt so humiliated. The gondolier had asked her for money. When the woman acted uncertain out of sheer shock and confusion, she had been dealt a slap on the face. She had tossed the money back at him and run. If she had known how to express her feelings she would have cried, kicked, and had a nervous breakdown. Perhaps she would have dissolved in the grief that settled in her heart. But now grief was tangible, a dark and hazy reality she would eventually adapt to.

And so she saw them, the pale-faced young musician and the red-cheeked whore with black curls. They giggled together joyfully as they headed towards the building that she had left a moment ago. So the deep melancholia in the young man's eyes was fake, because he could be captured by this girl's superficial mirth.

The woman was resting against the bridge railing. After she saw the young man and woman, her back became more hunched, her head hung even lower. She stood there like an empty bowl carved of bones.

She looked at the dark water underneath her. Filled with seaweed, stained with fuel. The evening was over and she turned off the city's lights… Later, in the obscure early morning lights, a few gondolas were visible then invisible, like ghosts ships.

If our story were written in the previous century, the woman wouldn't have been able to escape the sorrow that had settled in her heart, and would have given in to the dark call of the water. God knows when they'd find her body, tangled in seaweed…

# Fragile City

Suzan Samancı

*Translated by Alvin Parmar*

Diyarbakır groans under a sweltering heat. Over there, you can almost touch the heat, like string in your hand; it tangles. The Tigris is feeble, murky. On the other bank, impoverished, tired houses. A yellow desert drought in the plains after the harvest. But still, you can sense a subtle movement.

I am wandering through the streets of my city. On Stockholm's half-dark, sunless days, as I looked at the buildings with their pointy towers, the pines and spruces bent double under the weight of the snow, the serene blond faces toasting each other with a *skol* in dimly-lit bars, I would think of the full-beam, burning sun of my city, and I would shiver in pain. My heart would grow dark. Pacing through the streets like a wind-up robot, I would try to find a speck of trash. Those flawless parks everywhere I looked gave me such a sinking feeling... The sun I always longed for dazzles me; I squint half-blind like someone fair-skinned.

Faces, all bearing the mark of the same class, are nervous. Eyes flicker with pent-up angers, but are lifeless. A strange, mystical atmosphere behind a mysterious patriotism. The streets that at end of the working day become crowded one moment and then are deserted the next smell of dust. Between the trees, the hot vapor of the evening left over from the day. The old sign outside the Biz Bize restaurant. The men keep flicking their ashless cigarettes irritably. I go into a cafe that I know. The little white boats of my consciousness keep capsizing. An abstract fear inside me flares up again. People look on suspiciously. The desire to return to the fiery years of my youth is the desire of an excited child waking up inside me. For some reason, I was never able to be myself. I even looked for thrills, for loves that would give up on me. But I should have been myself.

One night fifteen years ago, we suddenly woke up to the sound of tanks. The rising metallic noises held all our dreams hostage. How awful to listen out for the sound of footsteps every night. The crickets, even the cicadas, had fallen silent. Artificial laughter would smother me; I would bury myself in the darkness. That was where I learned how to convert the fears silting up inside me into courage. Fears really do heighten some of the senses. Especially hearing and smelling.

My heart hurts in the stifling silence of this city that still, fifteen years later, does not show even normal development. There are still laments on the lips of people grown inured to their dead. In this city, love, hope have no color. The crazy tanks drive around. The sound of deaf jackboots. A yearning for peace and freedom drags you into the pincers of unease and uncertainty. What sort of thing is happiness? Nonsense! Will I never learn?

We learned how to fight in our mother's womb. We always longed to fly on the wings of doves. As we longed, so we gently rotted; the rotting turned into tides and later into waves. But we never wanted to be Nemesis...

Everything sheds its skin; there are more colicky spasms. I am tired of trying to be understood. An exaggerated sense of belonging. But I do not belong anywhere! I have no land; I have no people. At one time, I wandered these streets with the euphoria of unrequited love. While I was getting excited about changing the world, death was something very sweet and distant. Shouldn't we be careful about consciously believing that virtuous love is the best vaccine against aging? Now is the time of brothers and sisters dying, the time of fires. So terrible!

I want to feel the brightness of the morning sun. Let the flowers twinkling in the windows send specks of happiness into my heart, that is what I want.

What was my yearning for the sun? How sullen and stingy the sun was in Sweden. I want to look for the voice of hope in spite of those tired houses, the dirty yellow Tigris, those expressionless faces, that paralyzed life.

I absorbed with my hopes the night's treacherous bitterness as I looked at the lights of my city from the terrace of the Demir Hotel. I dreamt I was scrabbling around for crumbs of hope.

The freshness of the morning sent a breeze to my memories, which were waking up as I walked around the city walls. My childhood spent in poverty. How I used to cry for a *çiğ köfte* wrap. Pebbled open-air cinemas, roars of heartfelt laughter. Martial law, demonstrations, clenched fists, batons... Always the same cafes, contraband tea. How beautiful the exuberant green Tigris, the satisfied nights of poetry were back then. The feather-footed pigeons that cheerfully landed and flew off from the towers on the city walls I walked from end to end were still the same.

The sun is trying to reach as far as the Hevsel Gardens below. There is no sign of the picturesque horse-drawn carriages. The sign the local government put up saying no horse carts is fluttering. A little further along, in the non-Muslim cemetery, two cats are growling at each other.

And the tanks, which are a part of the day, go past. Then helicopters sweep down low over the city. As an old friend of mine, caught in the circle of paranoia, keeps turning to look over her shoulder; she hisses, spraying spit, "The only way to stay alive here is to isolate yourself and stop thinking." I look away and do not reply.

The tiredness of the inconstant night is still in my eyes. I go to a tea garden at the foot of the city walls. Beneath the rising heat, people whose fears were reflected in all their movements were helplessly drifting past like dead leaves.

The city would fall silent in the afternoon. As motionless, as eerie as a body swaying from the gallows. You could almost hear the cool murmur of the walls under the burning sun. My frozen heart, caught in dilemma, began to beat gently. My inner voice, deathly still for a while, started to send out shoots: I was wandering around in the garden of passions, sorrows and regrets. I followed the traces of the past again. When I woke up from my trance, the sun had set; I was drenched in sweat. A horse cart clattered brazenly past. Poor children who had been tipped off were lying in wait. Swearwords rang out in the hustle and bustle of the evening. I started to walk with a sense of not fitting in twisting around inside me.

The night was advancing, a heavy wave of fear was eating up the hot air. Even if all human values are locked up in the rumbling of this fear, we shall definitely learn that irresistible love once more. Our longings that drown under the shrewish waves wait for clearer days. And we shall definitely learn first how to make freedom bud inside us, and then how to look for it in the sky.

The stars sparkle among the stooping willow branches. An ignorant burst of laughter rings in my ears. I get annoyed. An emptiness, a loneliness...

The inconstant nights are not empty, I know; they produce killers, godlike.

As I wander about on the hotel terrace, I squeeze the iron railings as hard as I can. I feel like there is a feverish steam coming out of my mouth. Among the ivy, a night insect flies into my face. A cockerel working nights does a long opening number. Suddenly the sound of gunfire starts up in the distance. A red murkiness spreads through the darkness. The earth secretly wails for unnamed Hiroshimas…

I yearn for a real light that will illuminate the darkness of my city. And before you know it, an olive branch.

# Alte Liebe: Eine Kleine Nachtmusik

Tomris Uyar

*Translated by Alvin Parmar*

The day was at my fingertips like a piece of off-white paper waiting to be filled. Each time we got up from the small tables with their bright white linen tablecloths and their bright white linen napkins to look out of the window—or should I say porthole—at the misty lake that was gently rocking us, at the leaden sky, there was a different white. It was the beginning of a winter formed of the letters B E Y A Z, but that could just as easily be Y A Z, for instance, because it was only these letters that changed places with each lurch and jolt, and some of them disappeared in the play of memory, some in the play of the clouds[1]. (Or at least they did when you came.)

I noticed them when I was looking for a style of handwriting that would suit the day. They were mostly elderly. The women may have been in their eighties, but they were well-groomed. The wooden floor-boards creaked when they tottered onto the boat. They were taking off their hats and gloves, and sitting at their assigned places at the tables. At that moment, in the light reflected from the lake, the lifeless skin discernible through their thinned-out hair was raw white too. They had to walk along a damp, misty forest road—as did I—to get here. The

---

[1] *Beyaz* means "white" in Turkish, while *yaz* can mean either "summer" or "write".

branches of tired trees droop under the weight of the mist; in quivering droplets, leaves waft out a smell of resin, a smell of youth.

But here, inside, in keeping with its name, it smells of *alte Liebe*, old love: coffee, vanilla, chocolate, apple peel, cinnamon. They hesitated for a moment as they were walking down the narrow jetty stretching from the shore to the boat, and looked out over to the other side of the lake, nostrils twitching. Content to catch a faded image, the faint smell of something that does not exist anymore—a moment from the past? A face from the past? The past itself? I do not know if they found what they were looking for. The leaden lake shuddered, its waters started to unravel, the seaweed clinging to the pillars of the jetty rippled.

They entered proudly, silently, as if attending a ceremony; the wooden floorboards creaked. And when the boat listed slightly, they took the form of shaky, careful handwriting.

During this ceremony at least, in this imaginary refuge that had taken on a fully concrete reality because its unreality had been so masterfully played up, they did not have to compromise their Gothic lettering: apple tart, strong filter coffee. Their lips, waiting to be satisfied, half open like the lips of hungry babies reaching for the spoon, twitch and pucker with the pleasure given by a familiar flavor; they swallow. However, they cannot extend this period that has been gifted them as long as they would like. In a flash, they finish what is put in front of them. And as soon as they finish, their fingers, breaking the rules of good manners they learned from their families, freeze either on the handle of the china cup or on the cake crumbs that have fallen onto the linen tablecloth. They do not realize that they have cream and chocolate at the edges of their lips, which in their cracks have accumulated the cerise lipstick that could no longer be absorbed. Their hands, nails too painted cerise, which have served their purpose for now, are tense but motionless. While they wait, they listen to the small sprawling letters of Austrian waltzes that add a far-off tinge of majestic pink to the leaden sky—it is about to get dark—and the leaden structures of the city that they call "islands". Lake birds, lake animals glide contently on the water outside, hunting; they rise, rise and then dive. But inside, the young waitresses, their skin so limpid, their hair so blond, their bodies so healthy, all exaggerated as if to satisfy, satiate, rejuvenate these customers, wander between the tables in their spotless uniforms and with smiles plastered on their faces. A nursing home's kindly careworkers. Never really approaching the customers though, trying not to touch the cold hand of death.

The urgent gypsy music that replaces the waltzes just then reminds them (just in case!) that they need to go to the restroom before they get the check: the return journey is long; it has gotten cold. A burst of activity at the tables. Identical diamond rings on the fingers that reach out for the checks. No, not rings, medals. Prizes these women have won for coping with the absence of the loved ones they lost in the war, for staying standing in the face of so much pain.

The widows can also reach the level of chaste saints because the individual sexualities of those who died en masse in a war—heroes— were all melted down in the same pot, because they are already long since forgotten, because their bodies have returned to dust and earth and they have turned into one collective soul. From that saintly height, when they get up, they can bow elegantly to a husband left over from the war sitting at one of the tables next to them, and on their way out, they can bless them. "Foreigners" do not normally set foot here.


It was October 14th. The day after a normal day, that's all. I saw the others before you came. Two women: one twenty at most (how can I explain to you what this "at most" means?), the other one in her forties. The twenty-year-old was wearing a lilac blouse and jeans. The middle-aged woman, a pale blue sweater and a wide gray skirt. I must have been too busy looking at the people leaving to notice them come in and sit at the table that happened to be across from mine. Their voices rose, first separately and then together like two *saz*, and after meeting at the crescendo, descended into twittering. From time to time they fell silent, engrossed in the melancholy stillness of the lake. But it was as if they shared the same feeling, of this evening following the lake's tempo. It was obvious they had just met. Still, there was between them an air of being in the know that you find in people who have read the same book at different times, with the same excitement, and who have underlined the same passages in pencil. Or the chumminess of women who have fallen for the same man at different times and who now, unbeknownst to each other, know the same secrets about him. The twenty-year-old kept swimming and clinging to the shores of forty, while the middle-aged woman would suddenly swim out from her shore, and catch up with her in a timeless zone in the middle of the lake; then they would swim together, laughing, splashing each other; their laughter descended once more into twittering and subsided. As they could talk to each other even when they were saying nothing, in a sense they had been acquainted with each other for years. Even though I do not like wine, I ordered a glass of the same white wine that they were drinking. So now we were three. We smiled at each other when our eyes met.

A little later, when the day was purified of all its excesses and had taken on a contemporary sea-green color, you came in. In the present simple. Like an improvisation that had been slowly prepared through-out the day, that was awaited, that was known to be coming, yet that ended up being all the more surprising because it came at exactly the moment it was expected.

I had my back to the door. I read you in the surprise in the faces of the women across from me. You were the lead role in an old black-and-white film, a star who had made an impression on us. But you were him in his forties. That was the reason for the surprise. In reality, you ought to have been sixty years old by now.

You were still standing at the door when I turned around to look. You were rooted to the spot as if in shock. The piece of paper the day had put in front of me said that you had once had a relationship with one of these two women. But you strode straight over to my table, asked if you could join me and sat down opposite me. I chose to feign a subtle lack of interest by becoming engrossed in the magazine in my hand. Because after all you were tanned, the top three buttons of your white linen shirt were open, and around your neck, which was almost beautiful enough to make someone believe in the existence of God, you had a thick, matte gold chain. The others too had fallen silent: in your sea-soaked tobacco smell we heard the crescendo of violins, the untamedness of meadows, the neighing of white horses, all of which now could probably only be found in novels, and which for that reason had been abandoned, and which for that reason were never forgotten.

When you turned your head and asked the waitress for a cognac, I looked again at the muscles in your neck, at your gold chain; my teeth were set on edge. I sensed the danger: you were giving off a feeling that you might go, that you might go forever. A heroine of a novel written a century ago could, say, have thrown herself under a train because of that feeling. (She still would even if she were alive now.) "So it's not so easy to get over this romantic sickness," I thought. "And then in cities with a romantic past like this, it flares up again with a vengeance. If only we didn't have a language in common, if only we didn't have to spoil this moment with speaking."

But it was inevitable that you would speak: "Please don't get the wrong idea because I sat at your table. I'm not from around here. I'm Irish. I've been here for two years. I've been looking for this city. The Germans call this feeling *Zeitgeist*. I don't know if I've been influenced by films I've seen and books I've read. There isn't a restaurant, bar or den of iniquity—I work as a wine taster—that I haven't been into to find my city, but to no avail. I was just about to give up when I saw you from a distance. That's it, I said, the city I've been looking for! You are this city."

"But…"

"You're not German, I knew right away. Maybe it was your eyes, maybe your hair, maybe the way you hold your cigarette. Can we go and sit somewhere else, just the two of us, and talk for a couple of hours? Then I'll drop you off wherever your friends want."

The two women, who had been sitting there without saying anything for a while, without breaking the spell, asked for the check and got up. The twenty-year-old gave my arm a friendly squeeze as she went past; if I wanted, she was the friend I would meet in two hours. The one in her forties did not even say goodbye; she just nodded. We were alone.

"A cognac while we decide?"

"Of course. Look, I didn't get the wrong idea about you sitting here or about you wanting to talk… I'm leaving tomorrow anyway. My luggage is in another city."

"Tomorrow? Impossible, no! We've only just met! I can have your luggage brought here. I can have the date of your flight moved back two or three days."

"But you understand. Actually, I'm afraid, to tell the truth."

"And you think I'm not afraid?"

"Believe me, if you'd wanted something simpler, something more normal, I wouldn't have been so afraid. Talking is always dangerous. And it'll be tiring using a foreign language."

"There's a guest room in my house; let me take you there. You can speak your own language as much as you want. I'll listen, if you like, and try to understand."

"Two hours you said…"

"Yes, two hours. I didn't lie to you."

"You don't have to lie to any woman, you know that. Actually this city, the architecture too, gives me the creeps. That bridge over there, for instance; we learned that bridges are for bringing people together, but that bridge is for separating people, strangely enough. There are faded traces everywhere. In a city like this, how…"

"Can I not stake my past on a two-hour future?"

"We're both people who carry our past with us, we're of the same stock; that's why our conversation will get old very quickly and we'll get old and there's nothing we can do about it. I'd have liked to remember you with your brand newness, your foreignness, your unexpectedness."

"Alright, I take back what I said. We won't go anywhere else. We'll stay here and have another cognac each; we won't speak. Anyway, you've started seeing me as a person in a story. Give me a kiss when you get up so I'll stay alive in your memories. You kiss."

Then the notes and the letters, one by one, slowly melted. The people looking out the window were lost in the moonlight that turned the shadow bright white. Not a sound.

# Death in a Merciless Country

Mine Söğüt

*Translated by* İdil Aydoğan

I am dead, so they say. They're digging my grave outside as I speak. They say that I am dead. I've died and am being buried in this remote country. They say there are spectacular buildings in the leafy streets of this country, with flowers in the windowsills, joy and merrymaking on balconies. Before I died, I would gaze in awe at those windows and at the carefree lives led beyond them, at the colorful flowers hanging down from the balconies and peaceful sweet scents they diffused. There was a tall iron tower I used to climb to the top of and stare into the distance, as if by squinting hard enough I'd be able to see my own country. As if I'd fall into my old life if I flung myself down. I'd look into the distance with hope of seeing all I'd left behind. I was young when I died. A moment ago. They're digging my grave outside right now. This place was a foreign country. If only I'd never fled here. If the war had never broken out. If bright red cherries grew on trees all year round.

They've handed me a coffin. A stained birchwood coffin with a satin interior and all sorts of labels on it. "Put your favorite belongings in this," I was told. "You're going to be buried with them." "But I want to be buried in my own country," I told them. "The way it's done there. Just like they buried my mother and grandmother. Naked. In my *kafan*, washed and cleansed, smelling of heavenly flowers. In a Muslim ceme-tery," I told them. "Well, then you should've died in your own country," they said. "You died here, therefore you shall be buried somewhere here. Didn't you say you were an atheist? Now you're saying you want a Muslim burial. Come on, we haven't got all day. Fill that coffin up."

I wonder what I should put in this coffin. Would the railway tracks of the town I was born in fit inside it? I could squeeze in a bunch of redbuds from the playground of the school I went to. Then I want to take the ship in whose hold I traveled here. And a handful of corn. In memory of the golden corn that traveled with me, gushing out of the holes in its sacks at every wave and covering me. I mustn't forget to take a pair of shoes. The laced ones I wore throughout university. Their soles bearing the wear of all the roads I walked. A few love-makings, secret and rushed...

How am I supposed to fit my youth into this wooden coffin?

By the way, does anyone know how old I am now?

The priest says I would've been fifty if I'd lived. It has been a long time since I died. I came here when I was twenty. And I died shortly after. Leaving behind a village, a city, a school, an aged father and a newborn. I left behind a country in flames. We were poor. I went to school. I even got into university. But there I got involved in anarchy. I set cars on fire. Wrote on walls. I threw the soldiers from that continent on the other edge of the world into the sea. Gun in hand, I waged war in the streets. I stayed in hideouts. I was a militant. Then I became pregnant. Jumped on a ship and fled.

"Did I commit suicide?" I ask the priest. The priest is crossing him-self beside my coffin. "If I did, my funeral prayers wouldn't be said in my country. What about here? Do you say prayers here for those that have taken their own life, Father?"

The priest, with Marx's beard and Lenin's sparkle in his eyes, laughs. "You'd rather have died in the mountains, wouldn't you? You shouldn't have gotten pregnant then. You shouldn't have run away. You should have stayed in your land and fought."

"Perhaps I never wanted to die, Father. I never wanted to flee my country. Or come here. But I most certainly wanted to be a mother. To bear a child. To raise him not in my own country, but here. Where is the child I gave birth to now, Father? Does anyone know?"

"That child is now in the country you fled. He is lying on his back amid dumped rubbish, on a pavement in one of the streets of that huge city that no one in their right mind would enter. Needle marks and bruises on his arms. He's in a deep, deep sleep. He has dreams similar to those you had in the past. He sees himself travel here in a ship in his mother's womb. He sees his mother give birth to him in this country whose language he doesn't understand, in a temporary hostel. Then he sees her hang herself from a pipe in the bathroom of that hostel. Then he sees an old man picking him up from the orphanage and, after a bus journey that seemed forever, taking him back to his own country. He sees himself grow up among people who constantly weep, himself weeping constantly too. And just like you in your youth, he loves the streets. Not to fight, but to die. He has dreams, but these aren't of saving the world; they're of saving himself."

So I would be fifty if I had lived but I hung myself when I was twenty. They've been burying me all this time. Digging deep graves for me. They nail together fresh coffins that smell of wood. Here, in a country where I don't belong, they bury me, deeper and deeper each time. In this country whose language I don't speak, they mourn my death and pray. And together with me they bury an ideology, deeper and deeper. Over and over, in all different languages.

It was springtime when I died. That infamous wall was knocked down after I died. Hopes were dispersed. Losers scattered to the four corners of the earth, with no knowledge of what they had lost. I fled my country in a ship. And arrived here in a train. Through the hostel window I saw mesmerizing coffee shops, bridges carrying the weight of centuries, men and women ready to make love any minute, people swimming stark naked in rivers and singing beautifully, songs of freedom. I gave birth to my baby and died so he could live in this country in whose streets I didn't even have the guts to roam. I was only twenty.

Now and forever, they'll bury me. In this country where I never learned to speak its language, I never made love to a single man, I never swam in its rivers, I never went to its theaters, I never sat at its coffee shops. Deeper and deeper each time.

My father left my body here; he took my son and left. If you want to send me back one day, put all my remains in a bag and ship them off. I'll return from the country I snuck into as a parcel in a ship. My son can pick the parcel up. He'll embrace me and fall asleep one night. He'll bury me in a Muslim cemetery. Then he'll lie down on the fresh and moist mud. He'll role up his sleeve. Unable to find a vein, he'll try his ankles. No luck there either. As a last resort he'll lift his chin up and stretch the skin on his neck. His fingernails filled with dirt, he'll move his fingers over his neck. And jab the needle blindly into a vein his fingers will feel their way to find. And pass out.

And he'll dream of the country where he met life and death, where his mother is buried over and over. He'll dream of you, Father. He'll see you, and you won't seem familiar. Because he won't know Marx, and he'll never have seen Lenin. He'll never have seen his mother either, nor will he have ever hoped to. He won't have dreamt of beautiful days to come. When his eyes are shut he will have night terrors. He will see the country in which his mother gave birth to him and killed herself. In his dreams, lovers with forked tongues will make out in the winding depths of subway stations. Barefoot lunatics will climb up a metal tower, and barbed wires will wind around chairs of coffee shops. My son will hate this country. He'll hate the country he lives in too. Distances will mean nothing to him. He won't like countries that have murdered his mother. But they'll still be the poison flowing in his blood, shutting down each and every organ in his body one by one, the puke trickling down the corners of his mouth.

And didn't this country wrench me out of its system like puke and acid? Though I hadn't killed anyone. I, a harmless refugee, a revolutionary. I was just a young woman robbed of her ideals. I was only twenty. I was pregnant. They said I had to go back, Father. Back to my country. They open their arms wide to everyone, but they rejected me. They couldn't know that my father would kill me if I were to return with a babe in my arms. And ever since, they've been burying me. Deeper and deeper.

Years passed. My son grew up in the country I had fled. My father died. My son was on the verge of death. And I still hadn't been buried. The revolution had fallen through. Everything was nothing but a lie.

Now don't say words of prayer for me, Father; say words of damnation. Cursing all countries, the revolution and my father. Then hand me my coffin. I don't want to be buried here. I will emerge from the depths of the ground. I'll travel to an entirely different continent and lay in its soil. If I search hard enough, I'll be sure to find a merciful country somewhere. One that's nothing like yours or mine. I'll put my son in the coffin too. Together with my dead father and all unrealized old beliefs. I'll go. Some place far. To die again and be buried peacefully in a merciful country.

# Wandering through Snow and Desert

Handan Öztürk

*Translated by Alvin Parmar*

You die and come back to life a thousand times when you have been walking over an icy sea until dawn on a night when romanticism has reclined into melancholy. I am walking with feather-light softness over the snowflakes that do a thousand and one tricks in the sky as they fall to the ground. I press on without stopping although I am conscious that each step could be the one that does away with me in the mysterious darkness of the Baltic. Those feather-light steps of mine, instead of turning into Moses' staff and splitting the sea of ice down the middle and conveying me to the land of Canaan, are more likely to drive me into bondage in Egypt.

I am almost inebriated on the buzz of repeatedly managing to stay alive and the huge success I achieve with each small step I take in my battle of wills with death. And at that moment I notice that challenging death can become addictive. Instead of the terrifying cracking sound that I am expecting with each step, my steps are turning into a deep track in the ever-growing silence. My distinct footprints and the silence convert the night to morning.

I have stood up against not only social life, but the whole world, on this Scandinavian soil where rejection and the culture of rejection have reached their apogee, and now I challenge everyone.

I turned up drunk to my date with death. Alone and drunk. Confronting it on my own makes me unbelievably strong. And being drunk is my way of saying to hell with it all.

It is not pitch dark. Once the night has struck the snow-covered sea, it turns tawny.

The snow falls as though it believes it will ultimately be able to stop the savage wheel of the world from turning. It falls on all the nonsense a thousand years of human culture has churned out as if it wants to swallow up the unnecessary details. With a refined simplicity that manages to hide the mystery in their magical forms, the snowflakes fall, fall, fall… The whiteness, intensifying the sense of endlessness it creates, makes you feel that you are living somewhere fantastical. And the contrast when you come here after breaking free from the arms of an Egyptian lover who carried a mirage in his heart makes the effects of the ceaselessly falling snow seem all the more extraordinary.

When I leave the hotel sometime in the night and set off on one of my fugues, I suddenly find myself on the Baltic Sea. In my eyes, the bright white snow piles danger upon danger on the sea, the place of stories of fishermen who go out to fish and vanish in the furious waves, the place of ruthless imperialist wars. First I take a few tourist steps. Then, then I come face to face with the dark, terrifying ways of dying that these steps of mine will probably lead to. Inside me romanticism and death are dancing a savage dance. At first, I tempt death childishly. Then it turns into a shameless flirtation. I can feel life's most extreme contradiction on the back of my neck. But my timid steps disfigure nothing apart from the snow that I crush.

No cracking or breaking!

There could be just one crack lying in wait to carry me away in the frenzied currents flowing beneath my steps! I have no idea where this strange contrarian mindset came from and found me. Or rather, I do not want to concern myself with that side of things. I am focused entirely on the steps I take and on that crack that throbs in my brain even though I do not hear it outside.

Still, this is one of my happy days. I still carry in my heart all the savors and intoxications that Cairo has to offer a lover. I have Nefertiti's crown on my head, the sand of the boundless deserts on my feet. Medieval gifts from a modern prince. Maybe that is why fresh memories of love flow into me like the Nile in every romantic song, in every romantic place. Simple, unquestioning and uncaught in the trap of consciousness! Maybe it is just my way of frolicking with the insulated and isolated life of the North that I am encountering right after the specifically Eastern chaotic exuberance of Cairo, its crowds that can swallow you up and its heat that envelops you in a trice.

It must be that!

As I go down the road, I see people sitting alone at tables in bars; their inward-looking glances trigger this playfulness in me.

My pocket is full of lonely glances.

Their knack for rebuffing any of my glances that impinge upon their territory is so masterful too! Perhaps I should learn how to look so inside myself as well... I have to rein in my heart, my madness, my talkativeness, my curiosity for the life stories—intimately entwined with the questions that can be asked over a short space of time—of two strangers who find themselves next to each other, my enthusiasm that overflows childishly, impertinently. After the first impish greeting, the questions ranging one after the other—where are you from? what is your job? which family, which neighborhood are you from?— are enough to make me forget my city manners in an instant. Even that first reckless hello can be considered the first sin.

I need to cover up my soul. But there is no problem with my body. I can open its private curtains.

Another of the basic differences for women on streets in the East and in the West has just struck me in the face, and this simple question comes to mind: Is the East the paradise of feelings, of passions, and the West of the mind and the body?

I was careful to hide my breasts, my hips and my legs from the people swarming over the bridges over the Nile. But in these realms, I hide my heart and my passion.

Cool... cool. You must be cool!

Although the animal inside me has thrown aside mechanisms of consciousness and knowledge and has been released onto the snow, a dangerous boundary an amateur traveler like me will never be able to notice has already been crossed; I am walking alone in the sea of snow.

The lights of an island are shining on the other side. Disorderly and unassuming.

Its unassuming nature appeals to me. It suddenly becomes a destination. The masochistic game with death loses all its appeal. I change course for the island that looms like a fata morgana on the horizon. Now that I have a destination my steps are more assured. I am speeding up. A potential crack would now come as a surprise to me. Perhaps soon I will have completely forgotten about them.

My masochistic feeling is replaced with a related feeling: it turns into a provocative hedonism. I am one of those unfortunates who learned in adolescence that both feelings are a revolt against death.

Maybe that is why I can go from one extreme to the other as softly as the obedient snowflakes.

I still have an endless journey by dog sled on my hedonistic to-do list.

Traveler...

My!

Personality...

Way of life.

And desire!

The other things on the list, though, are just the first things that come to mind when you think of the North.

On the island, only the streetlights are on.

In the daylight that is slowly dawning and the whiteness that has been swallowed up on all sides, they look like they have been put there by mistake. I can identify with them.

In spite of this, my hedonistic perceptions are wide awake. My senses too...

I sniff the air. I am looking for steamy, misty scents covered in a sheen of sweat in the limpid air. My perceptions and senses charge in all directions at the same time with the hasty pragmatism of the common or garden tourist. They are on the trail of the dissolute scents I shall add to the past and to my stories.

The distant sound of an engine seems like it will bring me what I am looking for. It advances, slicing into the ice that has broken up into snowball-sized pieces on the route. The very much living water that appears amidst the snow whipped up left and right as the rear propeller speeds up is the only clue that it is traveling on a sea.

A traveler who did not look behind could not help but feel that they were traveling in a sea of snowballs.

I am a foreigner. Someone born and bred on this land that the snows have swallowed, when faced with a boundless desert, would have the impression that the world has suddenly become extraordinary; I am experiencing the opposite impression.

I notice that the different faces of nature have estranged people from each other at least as much as cultures have. Never mind that, when it comes to nature, the brain insists on looking for something familiar. The astonishments and differences of desert tribes and Arctic tribes vanish on the boundless white horizon together with this observation of mine.

And me, I have long since forgotten the land where I was born; and my country, I deliberately lost it.

I am where I am today, and tomorrow, I shall be in another realm...

The approaching ferry drops off a group of high school students and takes on a few islanders who are waiting. A young girl who just manages to make it in time holds her red shiny bag with care as if it contains all the world's riches, fashions and trends. But she has the serenity and simplicity peculiar to islanders in her still sleepy eyes.

I suddenly recall my life on the Princes' Islands in Istanbul. My days on Heybeliada, where I confined myself for years. The distance that I put between myself and the foreigners going past my house, the one-day tourists who brush past the pieces of wisdom I arrived at in the forests and on the wild coasts where I would disappear, my islander nature that swaps places with a teenage girl rushing off with untrained steps to mingle with urban life. Our glances meet for a moment. As an islander who has learned very well how to reject, I am ready to be rejected. She manages to catch the ferry; she carefully opens her bag, takes out her mirror and looks at herself. As the ferry goes off, slicing through the snow, the glint of her red bag stays with me. In my eyes, it turns into a symbol of the modern life she was hurrying off to join. It is full of dreams and hopes.

The students disembark noisily. The rhythm of the island's sounds has suddenly changed. I decide to tag along behind them. They go into the museum. Living history lessons. Attempts to raise awareness of the extended European family as per the requirements of Europe's aging culture are reflected on the museum walls. The voice of the teachers telling them about the history of Northern Europe shatters the spirit of the ancient artifacts in the museum. Awareness of the nuclear family vanishes among wounded Europe's dreams of founding an extended family.

I stop following the students and leave the museum. I select a small trail and start walking. The aesthetic of the curves of the igloo-like buildings topped with snow stops me in my tracks from time to time. One or two doors opening, the odd islander that comes out darts annoyed glances and turns inwards as though it is the same foreigner who goes past every day.

To turn inwards!

Inward journeys destined to run up against the hard boundaries of positivism. Travelers who ultimately turn every journey lacking in passion into a desert...

The sound of a flute suddenly comes out of nowhere, spreads like a spell and takes the island in its palm. I can tell that it is a children's song from the melody. It is obvious that a small child is playing. The notes, with a playful simplicity that has not been stained with intelligence, mingle with the snowflakes and add an innocent magic to the atmosphere. They awaken a romanticism specific to that person in everyone they reach. They suddenly turn this small Scandinavian island into the island where I lived for many years. I remember the bugle calls from the students at the naval school in the forest where I would go to gather mushrooms and pinecones. By manifesting itself as music, the classic magic of islands will grip me, maybe the students in the museum and even their teachers, and everyone who will come to and go from the island. I want to lose myself in these naive melodies with the pleasure of knowing that music has a completely different aura on an island, and therefore a completely different effect. It has an effect that deepens the sea, the waves, the wind, the rustlings of trees and the melodies of long silences that interrupt them! Faced with music that an island has imbued with a completely different magic, no one is anyone's image object anymore, islander or foreigner. Glances become sincere and familiar; mutual smiles are given away for free.

The snobbish mindset I am in, interrogating and judging every-thing remorselessly, suddenly descends onto my shoulders like a hump. I have to shake off this mindset; it is beginning to get uncomfortable!

With one final push, I climb up the hill I had my eye on. The pleas-ant warmth of the shining sun loosens me up. On this side of the hill, the snows must have been defeated by the sun because the sea stirs sparklingly, completed with the image of it in me. The patchy snow here and there does not awaken any illusions or associations in me this time.

I flop down onto some snow. I spread out my arms and legs and listen to the music, engrossed in the view of the islands large and small sprinkled here and there on the boundless sea, and of Helsinki faintly shimmering, as if in a landscape swallowed up by the mists. Once the music has come to an end, on the spur of the moment I sink my hands into the snow. I can smell the soil. The smell of exiled shoots sprouting from deep down…

I want to sleep. To sleep like this with my arms and legs spread wide out…

And I want to dream about poppy fields.

I abandon myself to the smell of the spring.

# Am I Going to Grow Old in Berlin?

Aysel Özakın

*Translated by Alvin Parmar*

The letter's franked "Büyükada"… I'm in Berlin. Cars flow past my window. Leaden apartment blocks rise up directly opposite me. I can't conceive who might live in them, how they might live in them, what might make them happy, what they might get angry about. Coming to live in a foreign country is a bit like being born and having to grow up again. At first you can't take anything in, you can't understand anything. Then, as the days go by, the meaning in the buildings, the colors, the faces of the city and the pace of life begin to come into focus.

The letter from "Büyükada" in my hand… Pine forests, old wooden buildings, the monastery on the hill, cafes on the seafront, cats, seagulls, a ship coming in. It's as though it's Büyükada I'm holding in my hand, not an envelope. A green almond; I'm squeezing it in my hot palm full of longing…

Summers on Büyükada belonged to people who liked making noise and showing off. But winter belonged to us, the people who didn't have another house in the city. At the beginning of October, the summer residents, now migrating to their warm, comfortable houses in the city, would ship their stuff out. We were happy to see them go, but at the same time we braced ourselves for the sadness of the winter months.

The last ferry would leave at eight thirty in the evening. Every one living on Büyükada would feel its departure with the brittleness of a child locked in a room. The lit-up white boat would leave us on the island's stark slopes and go. We'd be left in the middle of the sea, feeling estranged from the whole world, with only the seagulls for company. People like me who lived on their own would feel it the most. My ears would prick up at the slightest sound in the street. There they were, bringing the semi-feral *yılkı* horses down from the hill for the winter season. Even when it was very cold, I could never resist and I'd go out onto the balcony. I'd look at the horses. They'd go by in the glow of the streetlights, in the drizzle, tired, slowly shaking their manes.

I opened the envelope. I'm in Berlin. I've forgiven the island all its faults. All the sorrow it gave me; the boats that didn't depart when it was too windy or foggy; the flocks of seagulls that woke me up; my cold house, the smallest one on the whole island; the melancholics and suicides; I've forgiven everything. I'm in Berlin. I miss the sun.

The letter was from Melike. She was telling me about her day. She'd been to the market, she'd put some spinach on to cook. She was waiting for her son to come home from school and putting wood in the stove. She'd already gone through more than half of the six loads she'd bought at the start of winter, and like everything else, the price of firewood had rocketed too. Tension was rising and Danay had died.

"Danay's dead." My nearest neighbor, the closest light to me at night, the person on the island who had suffered the most disappointments, "Danay's dead"! How can these two words be enough to make me believe she's really dead? It suddenly seems that saying "Danay's dead" is like saying the island's dead. The days she went into Istanbul, she'd wear one of her old berets and put lipstick on. It was always because of money problems. She'd be going to sell a piece of her antique furniture, or to ask a foreign consulate if they needed a typist. Because their only income was in the summer, when they crammed into one room and rented out the rest of their wooden house.

I couldn't take my eyes off those two words. I hadn't even sent her a postcard from Berlin. I suddenly felt that was why she'd died. I'd become her closest friend. Now I'd never be able to tell her I was sorry. She'd gone, taking the offense with her. She was born on the island, and at the age of fifty-one she had died on the island. Maybe I'll go back one day in the future. Other people will have moved into the small house I used to live in. I'll go to the Greek cemetery. I'll look for Danay.

I'm looking out at the cloudy sky. The days and nights in Berlin seem to flow past me, independently. I can't get a purchase on them. I didn't bring anything with me when I came here, but I carried the faces, the voices of Turkey; I look at them, I listen to them every day. And here's Danay's voice coming from the island to Berlin. She's singing a song in her ageless, raw voice. An old French song... Her dark eyes, always timid and anxious, soften with the song. Her own voice soothes her. She went to a French middle school; she knows Lamartine, Alfred de Musset. You could say that's the source of all her pain. A life of poverty and drudgery spent looking after her elderly mother and her sick husband kept her apart from the poets and songs she knew when she was young. She'd sigh as she looked at my typewriter: "Yes, I know you've got troubles too, my friend, but at least you're doing something beautiful. I'm a prisoner."

I'm crying because she's dead. I can see her standing by the stove in her gloomy, cold, old kitchen. Drawing water from the tank in the garden. In the small room with her mother in one bed and her husband in another. At the tiled stove, sorting through the herbs she'd picked on the hills… Her husband watches the ceiling with his frozen blue stare; she strokes him on the head. No one can save her from living for these two invalids.

I took her a Turkish translation of a book by Seferis. She put on the black-framed glasses she had somehow never been able to replace, and a shy, touched expression filled her face. She had difficulty reading Turkish even though she was born and raised in Turkey. That would have been reason enough to find her odd. She knew French and English, but hadn't bothered with Turkish. Maybe she too had been infected with nationalist feelings, the scourge of the world, but she was entitled to learn or not learn whatever languages she wanted to and I didn't ask her about it.

She liked walking around the island with me. She'd take me by the arm when we went down to the harbor or when we went to the market together. It was like she was making an effort to show everyone how close we were. I think she was ashamed of being an unhappy Greek woman with a sick husband. She thought the greengrocer, the shop-keeper, even the fishermen looked down on her. And when we bumped into any of her Greek acquaintances, she wanted to show them we were friends. I was the person she felt safest revealing her secrets to. And she would complain to me bitterly about her Greek friends who lived their own comfortable, secluded lives without ever giving her a second thought.

If I'd sent her a postcard from Berlin, she'd have put it on the radio, no doubt about it. She'd have shown it to anyone who came to the house. Now I feel she was so devastated by my inconstancy she dropped dead. Some of her old school friends had moved to Greece. And some of them moved to Istanbul in winter. Among the Greek women I knew, none were as poor as her. She hadn't been able to buy a TV even though she really wanted one. She didn't even have a washing machine; she'd do all her laundry by hand. She'd inherited a piece of land from her father but she couldn't do anything with it. She didn't have the right to build on it and she couldn't even hire a lawyer. It was right next to the house I lived in, and in spring it would be filled with wild grasses in all shades of green. Sheep and horses would often get in and graze there. Danay would get angry and she'd tie up the panels of the wooden gate with wire. She wanted to use the wild grass for salad and *börek*. But the wire often came undone and the sheep would be grazing there again. She knew who owned these sheep. "Hacı Baba's son," she used to say. Hacı Baba owned two shops and one cafe. When he arrived on the island many moons ago, he was poor and worked as a gardener, but then he snapped up at rock-bottom prices the houses of some of the Greeks who were leaving Turkey. Danay used to say he hadn't even paid some of them. She knew how quite a few of the property owners on the island had made their money. She knew about their dirty tricks and the lengths they would go to, to make a fast buck. Sometimes I would try to talk to Danay about her own situation. I thought she'd be able to cope better.

"In the summer, they come out on stage, and we wait in the wings," she used to say, pointing at the summer residents who liked making noise and showing off.

And when food prices rose, I'd often hear about it from her: "Do you know how much white cheese has gone up? We won't even be able to eat it now, my friend."

She'd go to church on Sunday mornings. Leaving behind the gloom, the sickness and the poverty at home, she'd put on her classic black coat, a gold pin in her collar and a gray beret on her head. She'd put kohl on her eyes and wear lipstick. For some reason, on mornings she was dolled up, she'd call up to me from the street. I'd go out onto the balcony and ask her what she wanted. She'd say, "How are you?" and smile. I'd tell her she was pretty. She hadn't known any man other than her husband, and he had been ill for years. No cure. She was fifty-one and a virgin. I didn't like to ask her about it. She was emotional and embarrassed. "Haven't you ever loved another man? Did you never fall in love when you were growing up, Danay?" Why didn't I dig up her secrets? Why hadn't I gotten to know her better?

I can see her walking towards the harbor carrying a plate wrapped up in paper. There was a narrow-fronted two-story house squeezed in-between the restaurants on the seafront, and Madame Lili lived on the top floor. I know her from what Danay used to tell me. She was eighty-six and completely blind. She had left Russia with her family, but now there was no one left.

Madame Lili was optimistic and cultured. She consoled Danay; she would tell her that there were very great unhappinesses in the world. They spoke French together. Madame Lili had read Tolstoy and Balzac. Danay would tell me she felt purified and fulfilled after she'd visited her. Madame Lili was like a saint in her eyes. But the landlord wanted to increase the rent on the house she had lived in for years. Danay went and spoke with him. Why had I never witnessed their solidarity, their conversations? I wonder which graveyard they'll put Madame Lili in. I wonder if there'll be anyone around to think of laying them side by side.

I left Turkey. I went away from Büyükada. The pressure, like a massive earthquake, was making me panic. Danay and Madame Lili lived on Büyükada. And me? I wonder, am I going to grow old in Berlin? Berlin? What does living in Berlin mean to someone used to sitting and reading on blue chairs in the sun on Büyükada? It's misty and cold here. I have to find work. I have to sort out a residence permit. Ah, Danay, you kept your pretty clothes, your valuable crystal in the cupboard. You didn't use them. Just like you couldn't use your emotions, your beautiful voice, the foreign languages you knew... And me, I'm quite a lot younger than you and I'm looking for a life without pressure. A life that's not encumbered with talents...

It can only be Danay knocking on my door at this hour. The last ferry from Istanbul arrived a long time ago. I open the door. Danay hands me some fragrant marmalade in a small china bowl. She's just made it. As if she wants to apologize for needing my friendship at this hour.

"Come in, Danay," I say.

Forgive me for not sending you a postcard from Berlin.

# Life under Surveillance

Gülten Dayıoğlu

*Translated by Alvin Parmar*

"It's good we came," said Mother. "I'd had it up to here with Germany the last few years. They made no secret of the fact they resented us being there. As if we were going to lick the ground beneath their feet! And then out-of-work Germans pinning all the blame on us. Like there'd be jobs flowing down the streets if we weren't there! Potential employers lining up around the block! But it makes no difference if we're there or not, you still have to move heaven and earth to get a good job!"

Father was cheerfully slurping the foamy coffee from his large china cup, enthusiastically backing up what his wife was saying.

"What do you mean, heaven and earth? You have to move heaven and earth and the seven circles of hell too to get a job! But we leapt at whatever we could find. And it's difficult to find a German Herr who likes working too. They turned up their noses at the dirty work that we rolled up our sleeves and got on with. And then they've got the nerve to say things like, 'Foreigners go home! Stop stealing German jobs!' So let's see what happens now! I'd like to see them try working in smelters that burn into your lungs like poison, in stinking garbage trucks, in mines where you're buried alive. Well, how about if all the foreigners got together and left their beloved Germany, let's see how they'd like it then! They'd fall flat on their—faces, I'm telling you!"

"It's too much!" said Mother. "I've had enough of Germans this and Germans that. Let's just think of it like a bad dream: we've woken up and now it's over. I hope the people still there wake up one day too."

"You're right, dear. We moan about Germany, but it's all we can talk about. But let's thank God and turn the page. But I don't think we'll be able to do that until we die. Germany's worked its way into our flesh, our blood, our breath. We'll keep going on and on about our life there like we're reciting our prayers."

As Father was saying this, something from years ago suddenly passed before his eyes: the day he went to Germany. He had set off with unbounded excitement and high hopes. Then he sent for his wife and daughter. They packed their daughter off to nursery school. A job was found for his wife. They joined forces and dived into work. They never even tried to have any more children because they thought it would tie them down. Now they had the occasional slight pang of regret. Before long, their daughter would get married and leave home, and they were afraid of being left all alone.

Father shook off his memories and started talking again to keep the conversation going: "We escaped, thank God! Anyone who doesn't just get up and leave needs their head examined. What about your brother, eh? He's turned out to be a real coward…"

"True," said Mother. "I don't know what's keeping him there. Is it worth so much hemming and hawing? It's not like he'd be moving to hell! At the end of the day, it's just going back to where you were born and bred. And what's Germany got that we haven't?"

"Nothing at all! Especially not if you've got some money in your pocket! But try telling that to him! He keeps asking about Turkey in all his letters. 'Tell me everything about your life there,' he says. But he really just wants to see if I regret coming back for good. But he can't ask straight out. He keeps pussyfooting around. I answer all his questions one by one and when the moment comes, I say I don't regret coming back, far from it, thank God I came back, but it's obvious he doesn't believe me, because he's at it again asking the same questions in his next letter."

"And it's obvious you're not giving him straight answers! Write everything properly and clearly so he's not left with any questions. The city's not like it used to be. A huge supermarket like Kaufhof even opened in the center. There used to be eight mosques; now there are twenty. We've got cinemas, bakeries selling fine white bread, butcher shops, clothing stores, pharmacies, hair salons, dry cleaners, a huge hospital twice as big as the old one, five separate maternity units, four high schools, two vocational schools, and primary schools everywhere you turn; we've even got nursery schools like there are in Germany. And I heard that some people have raised money to build a nursing home too. Tell him all of that. Oh, and tell him about how many fruits and vegetables there are in the market. I know he and his wife are dying to come back, but their kids are dragging their feet. Bless him, instead of sitting there and asking you questions, he should gather up his kids and come over to visit. He needs to see everything for himself. He hasn't visited here for years. It's not easy to explain all the developments and new things in a letter."

"Yeah, from what I can tell, he thinks it's still the same round here as it's always been. And then his kids grew up the way kids do in Germany, didn't they! He's secretly scared they wouldn't be able to adjust…"

"Well, he's right about that! People round here used to be so conservative! Everyone had their eye on everyone else. No matter what you did, someone would find something wrong with it and tongues would start to wag. And young people could hardly breathe without attracting attention. When we got engaged, I wanted to get our picture taken. My father, God rest his soul, was so scared of the gossip he got my aunt to tag along with us on our way to the photographer. Do you remember?"

"Of course I remember. If I'm honest, I can't say I was very impressed."

"Well, you weren't a local boy. How were you supposed to know what it was like here?"

"Darling, I was hardly going to have my wicked way with you at the photographer's!"

Husband and wife laughed together.

"If my father, God rest his soul, was still alive, he wouldn't believe his eyes. Nowadays even local girls wander around with practically nothing on. I used to wear a headscarf on my way to the institute. That's what everyone used to do. Have you forgotten Şükrü's Patisserie? You know, we met there once in secret when we were engaged."

"How could I forget! We were both shaking like leaves, thinking the police would burst in at any moment. The fear made the lemonade and cake get stuck in our throats. But now I look round the city center and see so many patisseries, snack bars and kebab restaurants that have opened up. Full of men and women sitting together. Everyone eating and drinking, laughing and chatting."

"It really upset me to see that a beer hall opened up where Şükrü's used to be."

"Oh, wait 'til you hear this then! A new one opened a few days ago on Hükümet Street. If you saw it, you'd think you were back in Germany. Well, they do say the owner worked over there. And can you guess what he called it?"

"How am I supposed to know, dear? I haven't been that way for the past few days."

"He's only gone and written 'Munich Beer Hall' in huge letters over the door."

"It's a crying shame. There wasn't a single beer hall here before we went to Germany. Now who knows how many there are…"

"At least ten," said Father. "I don't wander around too much, so I don't know where they are either. But they were talking about it in the shop the other day. A lot of people have come back from Germany in the last couple of years. Some came straight here, some tried their hometowns and villages first. And most of the new businesses opening in the city center belong to people who've come back from Germany apparently. There's one who's opened a bakery over where the copper market is. They say he bakes seven kinds of bread. And he's attracting a following, by all accounts. I'll go over one day and say hello. I feel like giving him a pat on the back."

"And it's not just men," said Mother. "I heard from Aunt Rukiye that women who've come back are opening businesses too. Some run childcare centers, some have hair salons. And there's even one who's opened a clinic down by the corn market. You just walk in and she'll take your blood pressure, patch up wounds, and give injections and things like that. According to Aunt Rukiye, it's a hive of activity. And there's another one, she only lives two streets down from us, who's got the latest model of knitting machine. She'll do sweaters, jackets, socks for you cheaply."

"You know, it really does make me happy to hear about them doing well for themselves. I just hope all their hard work won't be for nothing and they're not throwing their money away."

"It might make you happy, but Aunt Rukiye's furious about it. She keeps ranting and railing that the city was already full of outsiders who came to work in the new factories on the outskirts and who knew nothing about our traditions. She used to be annoyed at them for setting a bad example for local people and leading them astray, but now the city's so overrun with people from towns or villages or from Germany that there's almost no one left to lead astray."

"Your Aunt Rukiye doesn't live on the same planet as the rest of us. And God only knows what she would do if she ever actually saw Germany!"

"She doesn't need to. She already knows everything! I popped round the other day and she was very happy to see me. She thanked God. She started off by saying, 'I mention you in my prayers five times a day because you brought that delightful girl back without dragging her through the mud over there.' Then she talked about lots of her friends and relatives in Germany with children who have gone to the dogs and turned out bad. Whoever she talks about, she's got some Germany gossip about them like you wouldn't believe. She curses the ones who forgot their traditions and religion when they got there, and blesses and praises the ones who kept on the straight and narrow."

"Does she rant about your brother's family too?"

"Well, you know what she's like! She can't really stomach them. When he last came over five years ago, the whole family went to visit her. 'You shouldn't have bothered,' she said. 'Your wife and daughters have turned into heathens. They're no use nor ornament to anyone now.' And she's angry with us too. 'You've spoiled Güler. It's not right for you to spoil her so much just because she's an only child,' she says. According to her, people round here will be calling her a floozy behind her back. But that's just how she is, my bubbly little girl. And there's a tiny bit of German freedom too..."

"And thank God that's all there is. She was only knee-high when she went. How could anyone know all the sacrifices we made just so she wouldn't end up falling in with the wrong crowd and getting corrupted! You worked during the day; I worked at night. We never left her to her own devices. We always kept an eye on her. But she did go to German schools. She made German friends. Like they say, if you lie down with dogs, you get up with fleas. So it's only to be expected!"

"Hey! What's wrong with my Güler? She did lie down and get up with the Germans. But she never turned her back on us either. She memorized all the shorter surahs. She knows about Allah and the Prophet. My little girl's afraid of sin. She didn't carry on with anyone over there, thank God! She's lily white and untouched. I hope God makes the bitter old spinsters who want to fling mud at her eat their words. I hope the Lord makes all the bad things they say about her happen to them."

"Amen," said Father. "And if you ask me, most of them are taking it out on the girl because they're jealous of us. Well, we did manage to survive Germany without forgetting where we came from and we came back with our heads held high, didn't we? Back to the family home. And with our coffers filled too. We don't need anyone."

"And you setting up shop so quickly without letting anything get you down surprised them."

"With God's help. People coming back from Germany spend months running around trying to start their own businesses. Some manage. Some don't. And then there's the ones who are conned or cheated or bankrupted or fleeced or robbed too. Things went well for me, thank God."

Father's business really had gone well. When he was just back from Germany, one of the local shopkeepers called Beşir had put the word out that he wanted to sell the family shop that had made him a living for

years, along with its stock. His children had moved to Istanbul. And he
wanted to pack up and leave. He dreamt of setting up an import-export
business over there. The shop was right in the city center and piled high
with home appliances. No one local came forward with the money he
was asking, so he began looking out for people who'd come back from
Germany.

Within a month, Father had moved into Beşir's shop, like he'd been
a shopkeeper for donkey's years. In the past, if he had dreamt about
something like that, he would have woken up in a cold sweat. Before
going to Germany, he was a moldmaker in a roof-tile factory, a penniless outsider from a small town. He married a local barber's daughter.
His father-in-law had been a man of modest means. He did not move
in the same circles as shopkeepers like Beşir. Well, times had changed.
And now yesterday's factory worker was today's German Turk; he had
arrived and set himself up as boss in the shop that had belonged to
Beşir, one of pillars of the local community. He was right to count his
blessings.

For years they had put up with the trials and tribulations of living
in Germany, but in the end they had got their just desserts. They were
comfortable.

Father said, "It's good that things deteriorated in Germany and we
had to come back here for good! We'd never have thought of returning
ourselves otherwise. God bless the Germans. I've got a business here that
runs like clockwork, a house, nice things... And a daughter who can't
get enough of studying. She'll finish high school soon. And then hopefully she'll get into university. There'll be a handsome man. We'll marry
her off to someone who's been well brought up... Grandchildren..."

As he was saying all this, Mother took his cup and went into the
kitchen. They jumped when the bird sound of the doorbell suddenly

went off. Güler filled the room like a heart-warming, mild spring scene. Cheerful, excited, pretty.

"Hi, Dad! You're still here?"

"Don't ask, darling, after lunch your mother set a nice strong coffee down in front of me."

"What, like this, with lots of foam?"

"You got it!"

"And don't tell me, while you were drinking it, you got to talking?"

"Yes, that's exactly what happened. How did you guess?"

"Come on, Dad! It's no mystery! Don't I find you like this every day when I come home from school at lunchtime?"

"True, true, and I should be on my way. Oh, did you stop by the shop on your way?"

"Of course I did. Bahri was sitting in your chair looking very comfortable."

Mother came through. "Have a word with that boy, for God's sake! You can't have an employee sitting in the boss's chair!" she snapped.

"Come on, missus," said Father. "It's not like he's going to wear it out! He's a person too. Let him sit in it when I'm not there. I don't like throwing my weight around like that. Have you forgotten how sick we got of the Germans looking down on us?"

Mother, seeing that she was not going to get anywhere with Father, retorted, "Do what you want. The ignorant peasant, perch him on the table if you want."

Güler started to snicker. Her mother directed her anger at her: "And don't keep smirking for all the world to see! They say a woman laughing is a woman conquered. We're not in Germany anymore."

Güler was taken aback: "What? What do they say?"

"Round here they say a woman laughing is a woman conquered.

People think the worst of girls who are always laughing everywhere. Men expect things from girls who smile a lot, you understand?"

"Oh, Mom! Would you listen to yourself! Which century are we living in? Laughing and being conquered, as you call it, are two completely different things! Ideas like that died out in your time. And this isn't a village or a small town; it's a huge city. Everyone lives how they want to, like in a European city. They laugh, they talk."

Mother was still in a bad mood: "That's what you think. But it doesn't matter how much the city grows or how permissive people become, local people will still think the same way. Whatever they were yesterday, that's what they are today. Aunt Rukiye was saying..."

Güler's face clouded over: "Don't bring senile old Aunt Rukiye into things! She's still living in the last century. Whenever I visit her, she goes around giving me stupid advice like, 'Watch out, my girl, you need to be more dignified! Don't talk to anyone in the street. Don't say hello to anyone walking past you. Outsiders have flooded into the city. You can't tell who anyone really is. Who knows what could happen to you? Besides, they don't call people who've come back from Germany rowdies for nothing.' It's depressing. Remember I took some *aşure* over to her the other day? Do you know what she said to me?"

"Of course not, how am I supposed to know?" said Mother.

"'Güler, my girl, you're getting a little more beautiful each day. It's time I gave you to my grandson Sami.' Can you believe it? I didn't know if I should laugh or cry. And her grandson's still in the second year of high school. Me and my friends from school are like brothers and sisters. I wouldn't even think of going out with them, never mind marrying any of them. You know I had a lot of male friends at school in Germany. A few of them asked me out. But once I'd made it clear I didn't want to, they gave up. I can't get even think of going out with a school friend. The German boys respected me, but boys here are strange. Most of them, even if they don't say it straight out, are dying to go out with me. I can sense it. But I pretend not to understand. The other girls from Germany complain about it too. They say the boys are always hitting on them as well. They're sick! Just 'cause we've come back from Germany, it doesn't mean we're going to hang out with anyone who crosses our path, does it!"

Mother stood staring at her daughter in shock: "Why didn't you ever tell us any of this before?"

"I don't know, I thought maybe it just seemed that way to me, or maybe they get used to you after a while and stop trying to harass you, or they'd begin to act like friends. Anyway, I hate talking about things like this. But nothing's changed. They're always on the lookout for an opportunity, the boys. Still, if it was only them, things would be okay. But as I walk through the city center, even men dad's age eye me up strangely. Everything might be good back here in our own country, but *this* situation's really bad, Mom. I try not to take any notice, but if I'm honest, it makes me really uncomfortable!"

"You're right, darling. You're sixteen years old. But you've developed quickly; you look about twenty. You wear nice clothes. And you're pretty too! So it's only natural you'll catch people's eye! You're a clever girl. Even in Germany, you kept away from anything bad. But you need to watch your step here too. Don't let them muddy our name."

That was easy enough for Mother to say. But Güler really did have her work cut out. She was sixteen, but she was only in the second year of middle school. She had been put back two years because she had gone to school in Germany. As if that wasn't enough, they did not teach German at middle school. She had to start English again, and she resented that. They had opened something called a harmonization course, and her father had signed her up for it right away. But it was of no use to her. What were they going to harmonize with what, and who were they going to harmonize with who in three weeks anyway!

She did not speak Turkish particularly clearly either. Some students and teachers had a problem with that. Her Turkish teacher got annoyed at her slurring her words. He made her put an eraser under her tongue one day in one of his lessons. He took it upon himself to give her speaking exercises so she would pronounce her words clearly one by one. She had gotten so upset…

The school rules seemed very strict and oppressive compared to Germany. Don't do this, don't do that, this is forbidden, that is bad, it breaks such and such a rule! And then having to wear a black smock with a white collar really made Güler's blood boil. In Germany you went to school in your normal clothes. And it was fairly laid-back. It was not just your clothes; here they interfered with your hair, what you wore on your head, your eyebrows, your eyes, even the length of your nails. Güler found it all so strange. But she was making a real effort to conform.

Her mother and father doted on her. She did not want to upset them. She missed Germany and her German friends, who she really pined for. But most of all, she missed the freedom in Germany where you were not under surveillance. No one criticized anyone there because of how they dressed or behaved or thought or spoke. As long as you stayed within the law, you could live as you wished. And then there was going out too, boys and girls together. There was no question of anything like that here. Girls went out separately, boys went out separately. There were places where boys and girls could go and drink tea or coke or something together here. But her mother and father would not let her go to them. According to them, local girls did not frequent places like that. Only outsiders did.

The neighbor's daughters had invited her to gatherings at their house a few times. The first time, it was really interesting. The girls put some oriental music on and belly danced for hours. Güler did not know how to belly dance. She wanted to learn, so she joined in too. The girls gave her a detailed explanation of how to do it. They could dance very sensuously. And there was one of them, the girls called her "Dancing Sabahat", it was like she didn't have any bones in her body. When she was dancing, she was so flexible and she could shake every part of her body.

Then one day they took Güler to another girl's house. Once more, they released themselves to the dance altogether. Güler had never seen anything like it before. They had taken empty tea glasses with spoons in and wrapped them around their hips with muslin like a belt. When they began to writhe and dance with the music, the tea glasses made it sound like a party.

The spread of food put out at this "girls' day", which daughters of leading families had organized, surprised Güler as well. *Dolma* in olive oil, various kinds of *börek*, cookies, cakes, buns, *köfte*, *mantı*… She got to know quite a few kinds of food that she had never tasted in Germany. It was the same way the girls' mothers entertained themselves when they took it in turns to host each other.

After a few months, though, she had gotten bored of these all-girl gatherings with food and dancing. When she had nothing to do, she preferred to sit at home reading magazines from Germany, or she would watch a video. There was nothing like watching a good movie on video! The video sellers had foreign films that were similar to local ones. Sometimes, Güler would ask them for different films, but the video seller would brush her off, saying that he wouldn't be able to shift films like that here.

But in spite of all this, what upset Güler the most was that people looked at her as if she was loose. She could tell, but she preferred to pretend that she did not understand. Because there was nothing she could do. Secretly, she did not dislike the boys being after her and looking her up and down with eyes full of desire. But still, these feelings were not enough to wipe out her unease.

She did want to have male friends, like in Germany. She would have liked to hang around with boys as friends, talking and arguing. That was what she was used to. To keep away from boys as if they were horrible monsters seemed strange to her. The girls she knew avoided boys like the plague. In class, girls and boys sat in separate rows. During their break, they whiled away the time in separate playgrounds. And PE lessons were held in separate halls. Güler's school was the only mixed school in the city. The others were all single-sex. Her father had registered her for it because it was near their house.

Some of the teachers were very positive and modern. And some of them were cut from the same cloth as Aunt Rukiye. They would pick up on anything that caught their eye and keep criticizing the girls. Especially the girls from Germany. They thought their free behavior set a bad example to the other girls. It was something that was often brought up at teachers' meetings. The ones with harsh ideas about how to bring the students from Germany into line were in the majority. The constant advice on how to behave and the criticisms about frowning, staring, clothing, hair, eyebrows, nails, posture, laughing and speaking depressed Güler no end.

When she was joking with her friends at break time, she would suddenly feel an icy stare from one of the teachers descending upon her and her laughter would remain frozen on her lips. But in Germany, teachers did not pay attention to things like that. Quite the opposite. If there was something funny, they would join in laughing too. Güler would often ask herself why: why is our country like this? The other girls from Germany would also ask the people around them the same question at every opportunity.

Adults would shut them up by saying, "You can't compare Germany and here." And some of them, once the subject was opened, would launch into praise of Turks, Muslims, traditions, customs. They would extol Turkey's national virtues saying, "Our people is like this, our country is like that..." When she listened to things like this, Güler could not help thinking to herself, I guess the Germans don't know that's the sort of nation we are. If they did, how could they look down on us like they do?

She was always writing to two of her German friends. She even thought of inviting them to Turkey the next summer. The German girls asked her to describe where she lived in detail. They asked her about her life in Turkey. They were very curious about whether she would be able to fit in or not. Güler always wrote good things about her city, her country, its people, even about her school, her teachers and her friends.

Once she even thought about mentioning girls' day. But then she changed her mind. It would have hurt her pride to write that she was only allowed to spend time with other girls. And she did not write to her German friends that the men she knew, her family, her teachers, and the people in the neighborhood kept herself and the other girls from Germany under constant surveillance.

But she could not help writing about the interest that she got from the boys. "There are some good-looking boys after me. But I don't pay any attention to any of them!" she wrote. When one of her German friends wrote back asking if that meant she did not have a boyfriend,

Güler's heart sank. She thought it over long and hard, and weighed up the pros and cons. Then she made up an imaginary boyfriend. "Dear Hanna, I do have a boyfriend and he's so handsome!" she wrote and began talking about the sort of boy that Hanna would like.

This imaginary boy was at the vocational school. His family had come back from Germany too. They were madly in love with each other. Her mother and father did not approve, so she had to meet up with him in secret. They could be alone together in parks or in cafes. Hanna was enraptured by this secret romance. In every letter she kept asking Güler to send a photo of her boyfriend.

In fact, Güler did have a friend at the vocational school who had returned to Turkey with his family. From time to time, when they bumped into each other in the city center or wherever, they would exchange a few words. Because she knew him from Germany. But he was definitely not her boyfriend or anything. They were just friends. They shared each other's problems, to an extent. They complained to each other about the pressure they were under at school.

Ünal was his name. His Turkish was worse than Güler's. And that caused him lots of problems. He had difficulty following the Turkish lessons; he kept getting bad grades. And there was friction with his family too. He kept protesting that he could not live here. Like Güler, he was sick of all the things that were forbidden, the pressure, the criticism, the advice, the traditions.

Whenever Güler was going to open up to her mother and father, they would leap in and scold her saying, "You've got food on the table and a roof over your head. You never have to ask twice for anything. What else do you want?" So she felt better sharing her troubles with Ünal.

But the boys who followed her in the street were encouraged by seeing her exchanging brief words with Ünal. They would start harassing her and saying stupid things to her as soon as Ünal was out of sight. Güler was horrified by how shameless they were. Cutting in front of her going psst, psst out of the corner of their mouths, saying "You've got some for him but not for us?", bumping her with their shoulders, rubbing against her, knowing glances, winks. Sometimes she felt like laughing out loud and often she could not help herself and did openly laugh in their faces. But that only made them worse.

She got rid of some of them by directly telling them to get lost and she shook off others by pretending not to understand. Each day it would make her feel more and more depressed. And it did not help that she had secretly started to like one of the boys who was after her.

The boy she liked would also try to get close to her. But not brazenly. He would find various pretexts. Once he asked her the time on the way to school. Then he started following her into shops. He would watch her and she would not feel uncomfortable. When she noticed him, her heart would flutter.

One day, when she sensed that he was following her, she let her schoolbag slip from her arm. As she bent down to pick it up, he rushed to her aid. Just as she had been hoping. They smiled briefly but warmly at each other and looked into each other's eyes.

Another day they bumped into each other in the public library. They both wanted the same book. "You use it first. Then you can give it to me," said Selim. Güler turned bright red. She said thank you and took the book. She went into a corner and started doing her homework. Selim was waiting for her nearby, looking her over with fleeting glances. From time to time she looked over at him too. When their eyes met, they were both filled with an irresistible shiver of excitement.

He appeared a few days later when Güler was on her way back from school. He sidled up to her in the most crowded part of the city center. He slowly pushed an envelope into her hand. She did not make a sound. She ran home so she could read the letter as quickly as she could. All he had written was: "I really like you. If you like me too, could you come to Bal Patisserie tomorrow?" He had not even put his name on it.

Güler excitedly sat down to do her homework. Tomorrow could not come fast enough. When she got out of school, she first stopped at her father's shop to shake off anyone who might be following her. She stayed there for a while. Then she left and went straight to the patisserie. He was waiting there. Timidly they said hello. They started asking things like "How are you? How are your classes going?" And they gazed at each other in silence for a while. Then they shook hands and left, promising to meet in the same place the next week.

It did not take long for these patisserie meetings to be discovered. Her mother and father at home, and the teachers at school were so up in arms that Güler did not know what had hit her. All she could find to say in her defence was: "But I haven't done anything bad! Selim and I were just talking in public in the patisserie."

After she promised her family that she would never meet Selim again, the joy she got from life became fainter and fainter. The sparkle in her eyes dimmed. She stopped laughing and became silent. Her mother and father and her teachers interpreted this change to mean that she had seen the error of her ways. But she was actually trying to digest the pain of being separated from the boy who she loved in her tender young heart. And it was not easy at all.

When she and Selim met, they really had only talked about mundane things. The kind of conversation you can have with anyone. But when their eyes met as they were talking, Güler was captivated and enveloped by a delicious thrill. She so longed to see her boyfriend again, to be filled with those feelings and to overflow with excitement again!

In her letters to Hanna, she wrote down the thoughts she had about Selim day and night so vividly and enthusiastically it was as if they were really true.

Late one night, she was writing to Hanna again. She was going to mail the letter on her way home from school. The teacher called on her during math class. Güler took her book and went to the blackboard. She started trying to solve the problem. Suddenly her letter to Hanna's fell out from between the pages of the book. She anxiously bent down to pick it up, but the teacher got there first. As he was reading what was on the envelope, Güler tried to take the letter. The teacher was suspicious and moved it out of her reach, and when Güler persisted in trying to get the letter back, the teacher became even more suspicious. With a snort he tore open the envelope and read the whole letter. He blushed and scowled. He turned angrily to Güler. "Go and sit down. I want your parents in to see me tomorrow," he said.

From that day on, Güler was well and truly in the doghouse. Her friends had all sorts of wild theories about the letter. Most of them thought it was to Selim. At the same time, her mother and father and the teachers thought that the things she had written to Hanna were true. Güler could not make anyone believe that they had not actually happened and they were just things that she had imagined.

After this incident, the pressure from home, from school and from people she knew became even more unbearable. As the circle closed in on her, Güler sank ever deeper into depression. The smiley, cheerful, bubbly Güler of the past had gone; in her place was a sullen, ill-tempered, nervous girl. A cloud hung over her mother and father's lives as well as her own.

Her father could not concentrate on the shop or on profits anymore.

It was destroying him to see his only daughter going faster and faster downhill. For the first time he gave vent to what was gnawing away inside him: "Ah, if only we'd never come back!"

And Mother backed him up: "You're right. She was doing so well in Germany. And she wasn't carrying on with anyone. She was happy and healthy. But look at her now, she's like a wet hen. And we're being so hard on the poor thing. But that's how it is here. We reined her in so much, but now tongues are wagging more than ever. People's mouths aren't shirts that can be buttoned! They're practically branding our little girl as a hussy."

Güler, though, did not care if she was here or there, she was so weary of everything. There was no more writing to Hanna either. It was as if there had been a lamp shining brightly inside her, but someone had flicked the switch and turned it off.

Spring came. Because she had turned her back on everything and devoted herself to her studies, she was doing well at school. Her Turkish was much better too. She saw Selim for the first time in months at the May 19th celebrations for Youth and Sports Day. She lit up inside, her heart started to flutter with excitement again like it used to. When they came face to face, they could not speak for fear. They just looked into each other's eyes and sighed deeply.

Selim was from a local family. When the earlier incident was discovered, his grandfather and his father had taken him to one side. "Are you completely taken with that German girl? Come on, finish your studies first! And one day we'll take you by the hand and marry you off. We'll make sure we find you someone from, you know, one of the town's best families, someone with roots and a pedigree. But if you think you can take matters into your own hands, there'll be a falling out between us!" they warned. Selim had no other choice but to keep away from Güler.

But he loved her so much…

A picnic was being held by a nearby reservoir to celebrate the start of the school vacation. The students from all the schools in the city were bussed in. They spread out in the forest around the water. Güler and Selim met each other again there. At that moment, they both felt that an overwhelming force was drawing them towards each other. While everyone else was engrossed in the fun and games, they slipped away from their friends. They ran around the reservoir from separate directions. When they got to the other side, they were out of breath and flung into each other's arms. They stayed like that for a moment without saying anything.

They were startled by the sound of footsteps approaching and when they let go of each other, the situation they found themselves in made their blood run cold. They had been followed by the vice principal of Güler's school and the teacher who had confiscated the letter to Hanna. The two adults stood there looking at them in utter disgust!

Before long the principal turned up as well. Thinking of his own reputation, he did not want the incident to get out. He nervously whispered something to the vice principal, who then shot off like an arrow. The principal and the teacher kept Güler and Selim, who were frozen to the spot out of surprise and fear, under surveillance. Neither of them said a word to the young people during the short wait. The vice principal returned in the principal's car. Then the principal started speaking somewhat gently, "You've both been very naive. Güler obviously thought she was still in Germany. I hope there are no unpleasant consequences. Come on, get into the car and we'll be off!"

As the principal was finishing what he was saying, the vice principal shoved Güler and Selim into the car. They headed back towards the city together.

Güler felt like she had fallen prey to her worst demons. She thought of jumping out of the car into the lake and disappearing into its watery depths. But she could not move a muscle. And Selim was no better than she was. The weight of guilt seemed to have shrivelled him up where he was sitting. The angry faces of his father and grandfather kept passing before his eyes.

The principal drove straight to the public hospital.

Güler passed her virginity test. But she was never able to go to school or be among people again. Because of the depression she had sunken into, she was admitted to the local hospital at first. As the desired result was not obtained, her mother and father took her to the mental hospital in Istanbul.

# Stephan's Shop

**Feyza Hepçilingirler**

*Translated by Alvin Parmar*

"Let's go round sometime today and pick up your shoes from Stephan," said Faruk. "We can go after I've come back from the supermarket, if you like. Unless you've got other plans…"

What other plans am I going to have? I'm looking for a job, but I can't do it on my own. I always need Faruk to help me. When he's at work, I just sit around in the house. At least if I knew how to cook, there'd be some hot food waiting for him when he came home. But I don't have a clue when it comes to housework! I tidy things up a little, that's all! And then I wait for him. When he comes back, we can go out, we can look for work, he can call around, he can set up interviews… What kind of job am I going to do? I don't know that either. I've reached the point where I'll do whatever! Could I do whatever? I've got no choice. I don't have the luxury of being able to choose a good job and turn my nose up at a bad one. My wife's waiting for me to find work and send money as soon as I can. My dad's waiting for the money to pay off the debts that I left behind.

I'll work on a building site; I'll do the donkey work somewhere. I'll take any job where you don't need to know the language, but it's become like Turkey here too. The answer's the same wherever we go, wherever we apply: There's no work. And wouldn't you know, some do say things like, "There would have been something if you'd come last week," or "If only you'd stopped by yesterday." I feel I keep missing out on work by the skin of my teeth. But even if we had come last week, even if we had stopped in yesterday, it would have been the same story, I know.

I must have been very comfortable wearing Faruk's shoes this week; I'd totally forgotten that mine were being repaired. Anyway, they were old and they'd had a lot of wear. It was Faruk who noticed there was a hole in one of them and that the toe of the other one was about to go, and he suggested I get them repaired and borrow his in the meantime. "I've got other shoes, son. And look, our feet are the same size. Try them on!" he insisted.

It was one week ago we went to the cobbler together. Stephan had that hunger that you get when you haven't spoken to anyone for a long time; he fulfilled his daily need for chitchat with us. He and Faruk had obviously known each other for a pretty long time. They chatted for ages. Just small talk, according to Faruk. Since I didn't understand a word they were saying anyway, I stood there looking around.

I thought in Germany people threw their shoes out when they got old. When I was in Turkey, I used to hear that they even send their cars to the scrapyard after they've used them for four or five years. So I was thinking who bothers having their shoes repaired? It was strange to see a cobbler like we have back in Turkey.

Stephan's shop was like a huge eye that looks out onto the street but that shows its interior too. Shoes, knee boots, ankle boots were strewn behind the counter behind the window. Men's shoes, mostly black, were stuffed into plastic bags and piled up haphazardly. Colorful, shiny women's shoes with heels and without heels, with buckles, with bows filled the shelves on both sides of the shop from end to end. Stephan was wearing an apron that went down to his knees; it had turned into such a strange composition of blobs of dye and scratches that no one would be able to guess what color it had been originally.

The shop was very small; it narrowed off towards the back, where there was another section separated from the rest of the shop by a dirty curtain. First, a dog the size of a bear came out from under that curtain. Stephan was quick to introduce us to it. He told us what its name was, what breed it was, how old it was. He gave us quite a lot of information about it that we really didn't care about. He'd briefly stop talking to Faruk and say a few things to the dog, then he'd turn to Faruk and tell him what the dog had been saying.

The next time the curtain moved, a woman who was twice the size of Stephan could be seen. She was wearing a blue and green dress with big flowers on it. It wasn't like Stephan's apron; it was clean. She was his wife. Although he'd made sure to introduce us to his dog, Stephan didn't bother to do the same for his wife. She gave a half-hearted smile as if to say hello and moved off to one side. From the position her chubby legs were in, I figured there must have been a chair there that she was sitting on.

Until then, apart from things about the dog, Faruk hadn't translated very much of what they were saying, but at one point in the conversation he said, "See what he's saying?"

"What is he saying?" I asked.

"That they'll send us away first."

"Why would they send us away?"

"He's talking about the economic crisis," Faruk commented.

Stephan looked first at Faruk but mostly at me like we had "foreigner" written all over our faces. "You are foreigners, aren't you?"

Let's say he knew I was a foreigner because I was speaking in a language he didn't understand. But who knows how long he and Faruk have known each other. Faruk speaks German fluently; he's been here for thirty years. Does he still count him as a foreigner too?

"Was it us who set off the economic crisis?" I asked.

"No," answered Stephan. "You didn't set it off, but seeing even Germans can't find work, Angela Merkel will sacrifice foreigners first to prevent unemployment."

It was as if he and Chancellor Merkel had drawn up Germany's economic rescue package together. And not even she could be as sure as Stephan the Cobbler was that everything was going to turn out according to the plan that she herself had devised. He was talking like he knew more than he was letting on. The expression on his face was enough to make you think he'd gotten privileged information from Angela Merkel and he was basing everything he said on that. That's how convincing he was!

At that moment, I started thinking what I'd do in Turkey if they did send us back. He wouldn't speak so categorically if he didn't know something. How could I go back? How could I face it? And Faruk? He was in an even more difficult situation. He'd been stripped of his Turkish citizenship years ago. Everyone knows that people like him who try to return are arrested and thrown into jail at the border.

Thirty years ago he'd escaped on a fake passport and come here so he wouldn't have to go to prison. He'd told me about that adventure again just the night before Stephan was rattling on. He brought each moment of his terrifying escape to life for me. And he also relived those months, each second heavy with foreboding, in his family home in Ayvalık, where he'd gone to lie low when he found out that he was wanted after one of his friends had been caught and given his name.

As he was telling me about it, he wiped his eyes from time to time, trying to make sure I wouldn't notice.

As soon as he got there, he understood that your family home is definitely not safe if you're on the run, but it took him a long time to find a way out. For a while he moved around and stayed with different relatives. When he realized that wasn't going to work either, he made a drastic decision. He asked his big brother to get a passport. He was going to escape abroad using his brother's passport, taking advantage of the fact that they looked like each other.

In those days there were security and ID checks everywhere. He realized that what he was attempting could get his brother into trouble too, but there wasn't much else he could do. He was encouraged when his mother and father gave their blessing and his brother agreed. So he left Ayvalık with his brother's passport, under his brother's name, as his brother.

First, he crossed over to Lesbos with the help of his father's fishermen friends. He stayed there only a few weeks and he spent those few weeks on tenterhooks, constantly afraid he'd be caught and sent back. Anyway, he had no intention of staying on Lesbos and living out his life there; he was only using it as a stepping-stone to get to a country in Europe. And what really took his peace of mind away was that Lesbos was directly across the water from Ayvalık. As he thought about just how close Ayvalık was, he was seized with a foolish fear that someone looking over from Ayvalık would be able to see he was there.

Talking about it now, he says it was stupid, but who knows how he lived with that feeling in those days. Because the fact is, it could have come to light at any moment that the passport didn't belong to him and that he was a wanted fugitive. And when it did, it wouldn't just be him who'd have to face the consequences; his brother would have to as well. Aiding a known fugitive? Fraud? Who knows what they would have found to pin on his brother. Then his brother's wife and kids would be in a desperate situation on top of the desperate situation his mother and father were already in.

He was much more relaxed once he'd made it from Lesbos to Thessaloniki. At one point, he nearly changed his mind about going to Germany or France and seriously thought about staying in Thessaloniki permanently. He also had the chance to improve whatever Greek he had left over from his childhood in Ayvalık, thanks to conversations in a mixture of Turkish and Greek with some old Greeks who had left Turkey during the population exchange and who frequented the coffeehouse he was working in. He got so excited when he was telling me about it.

His color changed and his hands started to shake, though, when he was telling me about his journey to Germany: how he had his heart in his mouth at every border crossing on the train, how he was afraid everything would be discovered the moment anyone took a good look at his face, how he wanted to run away and hide in the restroom at each new checkpoint so he wouldn't have to go through the same fear again. Who knows what he must have gone through on that journey if it can still move him so much even after thirty years! And then Germany was another adventure…

That night he told me so vividly, with so much breathless energy about his time in the refugee camp waiting for his political asylum application to be accepted. He told me about the people he met there, people of different races, religions and languages who all prayed in their own religions and languages for the same thing, for their asylum applications to be granted and to save themselves from being sent back. He still keeps in touch with some of the people he got to know there. The Greek that he improved in Thessaloniki came in very handy while he was still learning German. He made as many Greek friends as Turkish friends over there, and they always treated him well. "Friendship that's reinforced with pain doesn't easily grow old," he said as he was telling me about that.

But the only thing I've taken away from my own dark days though is the fact that I have no friends. Maybe I didn't give anyone enough friendship myself; but as I was writhing in despair, never mind anyone to hold my hand, there wasn't even anyone there to point me in the right direction.

I'd never had friendship from anyone else like I've had from Faruk. He was the only person I knew in Germany. He was the first person who came, not to my mind, but to my mom's mind when I had run out of straws to clutch in Turkey. We talked about it a lot: maybe, maybe not. She told me just to write and ask. How ashamed I was writing that letter. I was asking for help from someone I wouldn't recognize if I bumped into him in the street. I was asking him if he'd accept me into his home, if he'd help me find a job.

Before then, Faruk had just been my mother's aunt's son. True, in his difficult times I was still a child; but even if I'd been an adult, I'd have probably thought he'd only make problems for me and wouldn't have given him the time of day. As a family, we thought of him as a "traitor" in those days. I remember like it was yesterday someone at home saying, "Who knows what he got mixed up in. Why else would they keep trying to lock him up?"

Gradually we came to understand that people like Faruk were one step ahead of us in loving their country, that when they did do things that got them into trouble, it was always to build a better future for their own people. But back then it was even dangerous to be related to Faruk. As our great aunt's house kept getting raided, my family would get angry with Faruk: "Look at the trouble he's caused his family!"

But what did Faruk do? When we cried for help, he wrote and sent a letter of invitation with his name, address and signature. That's how I ended up in Germany. I'm not one of his political friends. I've never had anything to do with politics. I'm a distant relative whose existence he was barely aware of. A distant relative who he last saw as a ten-year-old boy, whose name he'd more than likely forgotten. Still, he opened his home to me, he looked for jobs that I could do. He's making an effort for me, he's putting himself out. He's shared his house, his food, everything he has with me. Even his shoes...

Even though the tourist visa—I still had to jump through all sorts of hoops to get it in spite of the letter of invitation—made it possible for me to come here, it won't make it possible for me to find a job here or work here or earn money here. I knew that. I guessed I'd be faced with major difficulties. What I didn't know was what I'd do and where or how I'd find a job. I was prepared for the worst: Faruk could have regretted letting me into his home. After a couple of days, he could have started sulking and making me feel I had overstayed my welcome. If that happened, I was going to sleep on the street, in the parks. I wasn't going to go back. Never. Only if the police managed to catch me and throw me out, if things got that bad...

There's nothing else I can do. The financial crisis came along like it had just been waiting for me to open my shop. I was wiped out before it actually hit. Mere talk of it was enough. I just hadn't been able to find my footing yet. I was doing what I could to make a go of the business, but I was reeling. In the meantime, wouldn't you know it, Chinese goods flooded the market. Who'd go into a glassware shop now? I moved the stock into my house; at the cost of the wife moaning and groaning, a room in our tiny house was taken up by vases, tea glasses and china plates that no longer had any chance of being sold. My checks blew up in my face. I was up to my neck in debt. I had to find money to pay off my debts, but there was no money. I had to find a job, but there were no jobs. I burned my bridges and came to Germany. I can't go back. It's good I don't have any kids. Leaving them behind and coming would have just made things even worse.

I was just sitting there in front of the window. I jumped when I heard the key turning in the lock. Was it Faruk back already? That was quick! How long had I been sitting here? I got up. I should go and help him with the shopping bags. It was the very least I could do.

"You're back?" I said, just to say something.

"Yes, I'm back," he said. "And I've brought some good news with me too."

I looked at him carefully. He really was happy; his face was glowing.

"Good news?" I said. "Do you mean…"

"Yes," he said. "I've found you a job."

I forgot about the bags he was carrying and flung my arms around him.

"A job, eh? Good job, you. You're fantastic. You're the best!"

"Don't get too excited," he said. "It's only a small job. It doesn't pay well and it's tough, but hey, it's a job. For now. I noticed there was an ad in the supermarket window. They were looking for people. I asked them about it. They're looking for 'unskilled' workers to unload the crates of produce from the delivery trucks and take them into the ware-house, and anything else that comes in. I spoke to them; you could even say I accepted on your behalf. The pay's low. But like I said, it's just for now."

A job's a job. Does it matter if it's big or small? I'll carry things. I'll carry the world on my back. Just as long as I've got a job. I gave Faruk another hug. It was a while before it occurred to me to take the bags from him.

"We'll put them away later," he said. "But now, get ready and let's go. First we'll go to the supermarket. You're starting work tomorrow. Meet each other and get to know each other. And then we'll get your shoes from Stephan."

Two minutes later we were at the door. Tomorrow, eh? I was barely able to contain myself. It turned out the supermarket was very nearby. As soon as you rounded the corner, it was right there. It was good that it was big too. That meant there'd be a lot of work. It was going to be good. Everything was going to be very good.

Faruk introduced me to the man I'd be working under. He was stocky. Blue eyes, light brown hair. His face was bright red and he had a beer belly. Next to him, I was like a child. He gave me a slap on the back and smiled. That was a good sign. Faruk would tell me what they were saying later. What I could tell from the expression on his face was that the job was mine. We shook hands and left.

"You have to be here at six o'clock tomorrow morning. The delivery trucks come early. The other workers have the key. They'll open the warehouse and the store. The supermarket will give you lunch. He says you can relax in the back room when you don't have any work to do. But it'll be a little difficult to start work at six. What do you say?"

"It'll be fine, it'll be fine," I said. "I've been lazing around for ten days. It'll be good for me to start work before I forget how."

I'm willing to do it even if it's for peanuts. I'll work hard and get in their good books. Maybe they'll give me other things to do in other places. I'll get paid more. My dad will start to pay off my debts. I'll send money to Pakize. I'll go back to Turkey once my debts have been paid off. And if I really start to like it here? Not many people who manage to make a life for themselves here do go back. But maybe I will be able to get myself organized. Then I'll look for ways to get Pakize over here. The first thing I have to do for now though is learn the language. I won't get anywhere if I don't. I have to understand immediately what they're saying, what they want from me. From now on, I won't have Faruk at my side. I'm on my own. Maybe there'll be other Turks working in the supermarket. That would be really good. They can help me until I get my German up to scratch. I'll do my best too. Faruk brought me some books. I'll read them in the evening, like doing homework; I'll memorize them. There are language courses if that doesn't work. I'll sign up for one of them. I'll learn German in no time. And I'll be hearing German the whole day anyway. Isn't it doable? Am I that dense?

Stephan's shop is nearby. We go out of this road onto the other main road, and we're there. Walking distance. Faruk is telling me something on the way, but I'm too busy thinking about my new job to be able to listen to him. Tomorrow's a new day. Tomorrow's the first day of my new life. I'll hold my head up high. I'm already standing up straighter. I've got a spring in my step. Just think, how crushed I was as I skulked through these streets the last time we came here. I didn't even want to look around me. I stared straight ahead, my shoulders drooped. Helpless, needy, cap in hand, penniless... Now, I'm bursting with hope, overflowing with it; it's coolness and blueness will reach all the way to Turkey.

We got onto the main road. Stephan's shop? Wasn't it directly in front of us? In the same row as the hat shop and next to the stationery shop. A black shutter, like an eyelid, had come down over that huge eye that opened onto the road. The eye was closed. It doesn't look outside anymore; it doesn't show the inside anymore. But why? It's early to be shutting up shop. It was later when we came last time, and he was still open then. What could have happened? Had his dog died? Had his wife gotten ill? Or Stephan himself?

"I'll go and ask," said Faruk as he went into the stationery shop. I waited impatiently for him to come out. That Stephan had really annoyed me the last time, talking like he knows everything. Economic crisis this, they'll get rid of us first that. But then he's got it made, of course. We're the ones in the firing line. Like the crisis will be over and everyone will be happy if they show us the door. Like we're the only thing standing between them and happiness.

Faruk came out of the shop.

"What happened?" I asked anxiously. "Where is he? What's wrong with him? Is he ill?"

"He closed down," said Faruk. "Closed down for good."

"Closed down? But why?"

"Because of the financial crisis."

The financial crisis! I thought you said it was going to hit us first! You were wrong, Herr Stephan. You were dead wrong.

No, it's not that I don't feel sorry for him. He's like us, just trying to make a living. Poor. I wonder what's he going to do now, how's he going to make ends meet. But I can't help laughing when I remember him acting like he knew it all, like he was chief advisor to Angela Merkel. And Faruk joins in. Us two Turks splitting our sides in front of Stephan's closed shop.

After a while I remember my shoes.

"So what's going to happen to my shoes now?"

"Don't worry. They were old anyway," says Faruk. "You can buy some new ones. Have you forgotten already? You've got a job now."

# Down and Out in London

**Hatice Meryem**

*Translated by Alvin Parmar*

## I.

When he said "How do I know it's mine!" I broke out in a hot sweat. I stormed out and went to Taksim Square. I sat beneath the Monument of the Republic and began to cry. I cursed all the nights we made love. I resented having contorted myself into all those positions—*that were all very difficult*—just so he could get more pleasure! I got rid of the policemen in the square and head-scarved middle-aged women who came up to me to see if I needed any help, and called the hospital and my doctor and made an appointment for the next morning. It was a very difficult night. I had to keep stopping my hand from reaching for the phone to call the bastard.

Still, I woke up feeling okay the next morning. I was feeling strong for some reason. My body must have been releasing something so I would be able to cope with the pain, I guess. And you could even say I was happy, lying flat on my back on the gurney being wheeled towards the operating room. Soon I was going to have the last part of that bastard still inside me scraped out with a curette, and then I would be free of him forever. The nurse wheeling my gurney was smiling sweetly too. And so we got in the elevator to go down to the lower floor. There was an old woman standing inside. She suddenly put her hand on my forehead and asked me in a tender voice if I was in for an operation. It was as if my body, hidden beneath the white sheet, cracked down the middle! "No, for an abortion," I said in a shaky voice. Her jaw dropped. Ping, we reached our floor. The doors opened. As we were going down the empty corridor, I was crying but trying not to let the nurse see. Hot tears were running down my temples and going in my ears. The world seemed like hell.

## II.

Thinking slows you down and often leads you to wrong decisions. So I did not think too much. I made my decision. I was going to find a way to run off to London. I had not been educated in the Anglo-Saxon model, I did not know too much about London, and I did not know anyone there either, except for a friend of mine who had gone there a few months earlier. So I made a mental note to leave this city and go there because I hated my job, I was sick of my family's smothering rules and also because of my relationship that just did not seem to stay on track.

I worked three more months and saved up the money for the plane ticket. I got in touch with a Jewish family to stay with them as an au pair, and when the time came, I filled a suitcase with my clothes and books, and set off. While I was getting off the plane at Heathrow, I still could not believe what I was doing. I had run away from the man and the city that did not love me. A new life awaited me.

They had Israeli flags in their children's bedrooms, the Torah in their hands and many Hebrew tongue twisters in their speech. My whole life, I have never been able to escape from feeling that I have to please others. I began to learn Hebrew and read the Torah every day to please the children, the eldest of whom was twelve. I learned a lot of new things about where Israel was on the map, its geography, population, flora, army, lifestyle, traditions and customs. The Torah never ceased to amaze me. God, according to it, drew up the borders of Israel like a land registrar; he would tell the Jews that the land beyond such and such a river was theirs.

I would share the things I learned with the children. You could even say that I had become staunchly pro-Jewish. I hated the genocidal Germans. *Schindler's List* was my favorite film. But it turns out that the children got well and truly fed up with this religious and nationalist onslaught raining down on them! One day they screamed at me to my face that they did not like me at all. To their mother and father, though, I was the best thing since sliced bread. They kept saying that they had never seen an au pair like me. Like I said, pleasing others was my main function in life. Now, I would go above and beyond the call of duty so I could worm my way even further into their good books. One evening, they went out, leaving the children with me. The little girl had a bad cough. I grabbed my sleeping bag, spread it out in front of her door and fell asleep with a book in my hand. When the mother and father came home later on that night, you should have seen the look on their faces! They looked surprised and in awe at the same time as if they were beholding at a saint! They had tears in their eyes! Like I said, they could not praise me enough.

## III.

No one should ever go over the top with praising me; it just fills me with the desire to double-cross them. I do not know why. That is just how it is. My employers were astounded when I started coming home drunk in the wee hours and taking my time on my international phone calls. They had words with me. They asked me if I was depressed and said quite openly that they did not approve of what I was doing. I nodded like a sheep and told them they were right, but from that minute I was making my own plans. The next morning, I packed my bags and left without telling them. I knew what I was doing legally wrong; I realized I was leaving them in the lurch; I was sorry about that; it was not like I had anywhere to go, but I still left anyway.

## IV.

A friend in need is a friend indeed. A Turkish girl I knew from the school I went to supposedly to learn English said I could stay with her for a few days. I put a small card in the window of a supermarket: "Ironing and cleaning services offered."

Carla called me one week later. I went to meet her. She lived in a small stately home. She had a covered Olympic swimming pool and even a huge nine- or ten-person sauna in the back garden. She needed help urgently because she had just had triplets after her two sons. It was patently obvious that she was American trailer trash who had found a rich English husband and run off to London; she was also dazzlingly beautiful.

I moved into a small room next to the boys' room. One of them supported Galatasaray. He would reel off the names of the players one by one. Everyone in the house was competing with each other to see who could be the friendliest and nicest to me. They got a bike for me so I could easily get to the town center three or four kilometers away. Silly them! Like I said, you need to be careful about being too nice to me, you do not know what you are unleashing!

Carla got pregnant again a few weeks later. She kept burping; she kept drinking sparkling mineral water. She was going through a crate of the stuff a day. She had a huge bedroom. Big enough to fit the whole three-bedroom house my family and I lived in in Istanbul. There were wardrobes on every wall. In spite of that, she would still strew her knickers (pink ones, purple ones, black ones, cream ones of every shape and style) all over the room. She annoyed me.

Something strange happened one day. All of the telephones throughout our stately home suddenly started ringing and someone started pounding at the front door. I was running to the door with a duster in my hand when Carla blocked my way. We went upstairs together. We looked out of the window and she pointed to the stocky man at the door. He was shaking his fists and cursing: "I'll burn this bloody house down! Come out, you harlot! I'm the father of those triplets!"

God knows I was scared! I did not want to die as an au pair in this house just like that. I had dreams. I was going to travel the world.

Carla told me things like he would not leave her alone and she was scared of being killed if her husband found out.

Times like that bring out the worst in you even if you do not have a malicious bone in your body. I did not feel the slightest pang of conscience writing that letter to Carla's husband. The American slut was clearly cheating on the poor man. I put the letter on his desk and left.

## V.

In those days, there was only one thing au pairs in London dreamt of: becoming a lady! And as it was the sleaziest and cheapest way of making this dream come true, most of them were sleeping with English men. In truth, they too could not get enough of Turkish girls. Back then, most of them were virgins and very geisha-like in spirit. All they thought about was cooking breakfast and making coffee for their husbands every morning.

I started staying with a half-mad woman whose husband had left her and who was an aspiring writer. She would sit at her typewriter all night until morning and I could not get to sleep because of the noise. So I became a regular at a pub called The Stag. I would go back home very late. And all the au pairs in the area would hang out there too. There could be as many as ten or fifteen girls sitting at one table eying up all the red-faced, spotty English boys around. Czech, French, German, Macedonian, Croatian, Turkish… As far as I could tell, it did not matter which country they came from; they all had the same plans for the future. To be a lady!

I got to know someone called Kerem who worked in the chip shop in the same town. Turkish girls who lost all their inhibitions as soon as they got abroad pissed him off. I went to The Stag with him one evening. The au pairs were at the same table again. He had already met the three Turkish girls among them. We said hello and went and sat down at a small table.

A short while later, someone with a microphone burst onto the floor and announced that there was going to be a competition. The girls started shouting and screaming. Six chairs were placed next to each other in the space in front of the bar. Six English boys sat down on them and put the inflated balloons that had been thrust into their hands between their legs. To egg the girls on, the person with the microphone yelled, "The first person who bursts a balloon will get to take this cuddly stag home!" and held up a toy deer. But really there was no need for a prize; the girls were already fired up.

They snuggled on the boys' laps, some of them pretending to be reluctant, some of them positively going for it. When they started bouncing up and down accompanied by some fast-paced music, Kerem left, saying that it turned his stomach, that he could not bear to see Turkish girls acting like that. I stayed because I did not share the same nationalist point of view. I could not take my eyes off them. The balloons would just not burst no matter much the girls bounced; they were wiggling their bottoms determinedly, bringing them down; the young men were grinning with delight.

Do I need to mention that a Turkish girl—*who I later learnt that Kerem really liked*—won? We heard that she married an Englishman two months later, that she had become the lady of a two-story house with a garden, that she bought her food from the expensive supermarket in town and cooked breakfast and made coffee for her husband every morning. Kerem became an alcoholic.

## VI.

I never went to Madame Tussaud's or any other museums. It was my own sort of protest. Against cliché-ridden English culture, which seemed to me to get faker each day. I did not like their wealth or the way they paraded it. A discerning animosity was developing inside me. As if I wanted to find where they were defective, lacking. I would spend half my day doing temporary jobs like washing up somewhere or delivering newspapers; then I would wander aimlessly through the streets with a book of Orhan Veli's poetry in my hand. I had the convenience and inconvenience of not being officially registered. I would eat the cheapest kind of pizza or instant noodles when I got hungry. I was smoking a lot.

I was on one of the bridges over the Thames one day. I was walking. At the end of the bridge, I saw someone begging; he was tightly wrapped in a blue sleeping bag and had hunched his back. He looked down on his luck. As I went by, he asked me for money. I laughed. Then he asked me for a cigarette. I took out my packet and offered him one. He did not want to take it when he saw it was the last one. I insisted. We were off to a friendly start.

"Are you from round here?"

"I'm Scottish."

"What's your real job?"

"Painter decorator."

"Why don't you do that?"

"I earn more doing this."

"Is it legal?"

"We run away from the police."

"So I take it you earn a lot per day?"

"Eighty to a hundred pounds."

My eyes almost popped out of my head. "I want to be a beggar too," I said. As he was making up something about it being impossible, I saw a policeman below at the foot of the bridge. "What's your name?" I asked.

"Peter," he said.

"Well, Peter, there's a policeman down there!"

He leapt up and got out of the sleeping bag and folded it up. His misshapen form was suddenly gone. It turns out he was quite sprightly! "I want to be a beggar too," I said again.

"Meet me underneath the arches on Monday," he said as he was walking off.

I sat down on the crate he had left; I opened my book and started to read.

*No matter how beautiful the roads are, no matter how cool the night is,*
*the body tires, the headache does not. Even if I went home now, I might go*
*out a little later, seeing that these clothes and shoes belong to me, and seeing*
*that the streets belong to no one.*

I loved Orhan Veli.

# VII.

On Monday, I went underneath the arches. I had never been under
any bridges in Istanbul. A giant dog went for me. "Stop, Sasha!" yelled
a young Rasta. I asked him where Peter was. "Are you his girlfriend?"
he asked. I was surprised. "Peter's not here, but we are, come!" he said
and walked off.

I followed him with my eyes. I could see small huts made out of
cardboard boxes, men covered in grime and a large fire burning in the
middle. It was freezing. A sparkly world on that dark London day, I
thought. I walked up to them without hesitating.

The figures gathered around the fire looked like several creatures
that could no longer be called people. As well as the ones who looked
disabled and deformed, there was also a wild-eyed woman who I was
astounded to see half-naked in that cold. I sat down on a broken office
chair. I stretched out my hands to the fire to warm up. They were talking about Peter. He had toothache, he had gone to find medicine, he
would be back soon, and things like that. They were making fun of me
because they still thought I was his girlfriend.

A dark-haired, dark-eyed middle-aged man who had no legs but
who could get around on a plank with wheels asked me where I was
from. When I said I was Turkish, he started singing a well-known

Turkish song, "Üsküdar'a gider iken"! And next thing you know, there I was pining for Istanbul! The people I loved, the people I loathed, the people who loved me, the people who loathed me, its air, its water, its birds, absolutely everything. But most of all him! Places we had been together, islands, places like Moda, Beyoğlu, cinemas…

It turns out that that man with no legs was Italian. He had sailed to Istanbul, before he lost his legs. He said he liked the Turks. Someone else said that Turks could not be trusted and never kept their word. I pretended not to hear. We started talking about the homeless in London. It got more and more crowded around the fire. Some filthy nine- or ten-year-olds appeared like ghosts from somewhere and came over.

I thought I was in another city inside the city. It was the first time I had felt this good here. They were living illegally, they only worried about where their next meal was coming from, they did not belong to the world or to life flowing past. I was well and truly one of them.

Then they started asking me questions. So who was I? What was I doing there?

I told them I had studied human relations at university, that I had worked in an agency for three years, that I hated that job, that I dreamt of becoming a writer one day. When I saw they were listening with admiration and curiosity, I could not stop myself. I poured out my whole life story to them. I moaned about my obsessive-compulsive mother, about my conservative father, and most of all about my waste-of-space boyfriend. They all took my side. They even tried to comfort me. Not to mention that they were more offended than I was by my boyfriend saying "How do I know it's mine!"

Then a young German woman holding a baby came over from one of the cardboard-box huts. She fished out a potato that was falling apart in a tin can cooking on the fire and offered it to me; her hand was caked black with dirt. I was hungry. I took it without feeling disgust and popped it in my mouth.

Just then an elegant, well-groomed woman hurled a huge plastic bag down from the steep stairs that went up to the bridge. It landed right next to us. It turns out that rich Londoners bring clothes for the poor over Christmas. There was a long white fur coat in the bag. Sasha's owner could see that I was cold and he wrapped the coat around my shoulders. I sat with them until late into the night. When it was time to go, they insisted I keep the fur coat. They would not take no for an answer.

I walked towards the Underground in a long white fur coat thinking that the poor made the world richer.

# Take Courage, Tell This Story!

## Işıl Özgentürk

*Translated by Mark David Wyers*

There was this experience I had in Germany when I was younger and, until now, I have only told my closest friends about it because I was afraid people would say, "Oh, come on, Işıl, you're just spinning tales again." But let me tell you the story. The newspaper I was working for had sent me to Germany, but they booked my trip on a bus of illegal migrant workers. Thankfully, ever since I was a child I have always loved all sorts of travel, and I figured in any case I would get the scoop on some interesting issues along the way, and we set off. The story of this trip, however, is another tale altogether: how our bus was taken into a hangar and German shepherds were set upon us, how I shouted at a German police officer until he cowered in fear, how the fifteen illegal workers kneeled in prayer for me after we got through customs—but these are everyday things, let's get on with the plot.

In Germany I was working myself to the bone; as I think back on it, my mind swarms with the stories I heard and the things I saw, but I think I'll tell you the funniest and most surprising episode. As a side note, in those days when you traveled from Munich to Berlin by train, it had to pass through East Germany, and when it did, all of the train personnel were replaced by East Germans and all of the windows and doors were locked up tight so that nobody could escape, and it was during this part of the harrowing trip that I had to give a heroin injection in the neck of a man who was reading a German translation of Nazım Hikmet's poetry and who told me that he was going to die in three months; anyways I wrote about this in detail in my book *On an Enchanted Journey*, so I'll move on to the meat of the tale.

I was 26 years old then, which means it was 1973 and we had gotten through the worst of the military coup in Turkey, and as I am from the generation of '68, I had seen a lot of violence and upheaval in those years, so I thought I knew everything; I should point out that I have never been a moralist, and this is probably genetic, many thanks to my mother and father, and in short, having sex and falling in love were a part of my life at that time. I am not sure why I am telling you this, but be patient—in those days there was no internet and porn was just not that common. And there I was, thinking that I was so worldly but I had never seen a porno.

One time I crossed into East Germany and went to the horse races with some opposition painters and, lo and behold, I bet on a black horse and managed to pocket quite a bit of money, but when I tried to cross the border again, I was held until midnight because I had bought a stack of Bertolt Brecht books worth three times the money I had declared when entering. Other things were going on as well, and I was living it up; I was being invited by Alawi families to join in their worship ceremonies, and for the first time in my life, a lesbian hit on me, but of course I, who supposedly knew everything, had no idea she was interested in me until my friends pointed it out.

Bear with me, I am getting to the heart of the story; I had an Armenian friend who was a clever networker, and she had brought me glad tidings—six women staying at a local *Heim*, which are small housing units for laborers, had agreed to an interview. I was going to be able to ask them anything I wanted.

Hurrah, finally! I went to meet the women with my Armenian friend, a bouquet of flowers in hand, and we gathered in one of the rooms of the *Heim*, where a Turkish spread had been laid out, the likes of which I had never seen in Germany, replete with yogurt which they had made themselves, and my stomach growled at the sight of bulgur salad, stuffed vine leaves and white bean salad, and there was even a strong bottle of *rakı*.

We sat down to the meal with the six women, who came from all parts of Turkey; two were from the province of Erzincan in the poorer east of Turkey and had started working at the wire bending machines in a television factory, one was from the uplands of the Black Sea coast, one was from the village of Tokat in central Anatolia, another from the province of Hatay bordering Syria, and one was from a town in Kastamonu, and they were all chattering, complaining about Germany and about the fact that they missed their children. One of them said that she had made a tape recording and sent it to her child, another spoke of how she missed her fiancé, and another mentioned that she had acquired a local lover—she was the liveliest of the bunch and didn't mind showing off in front of the others.

We chatted about this and that, and finished the bottle of rakı, and then another bottle appeared, and the woman with the lover said, "Since you are going to write about our problems and the things we miss, we would like to do something for you." She went to a table in the corner of the room, removed the covering from a large box which I had thought was a television and pulled out an 8-millimeter film projector. After setting up the first movie, she turned off the lights and the film began to play, projected on the wall; at first I didn't understand what was going on but then it dawned on me that it was gay porn—how ignorant I was! I am ashamed to admit that I bolted for the restroom and vomited; anyone who knows me will tell you that I would never belittle anyone's sexual preferences, but I had never seen anything like that and was honestly quite shocked. I was young and oblivious; after I emerged from the restroom, the women were laughing, saying, "This little girl is a bit delicate."

As they tittered, the second film started, and that one was hetero porn, and I sat and watched it without batting an eyelash because they were all glancing at me to see my reaction. Then at one point, and I apologize for this (look at me, even now I am apologizing) the man and woman in the film started having anal sex, and the women in the *Heim* moaned, "Oooh, that hurts so much!" and went on about other ways of doing it, but the one with the lover chimed in, "Not at all, if you get used to it, anal is even sweeter than doing it the other way!"

Then that film finished and another started, it was a cartoon porno in which Tarzan was swinging from branch to branch from his extraordinarily long penis, bellowing "Ahahahaaaaaha." I was about to split my sides I laughed so hard.

I won't drag it out, but I am grateful for the education that this 26 year-old woman from the generation of '68 received in the *Heim* that day. Thanks to those women, and I hope life has blessed them with happiness.

Well, it is out in the open now, just how green I was; well, a story is a story, there it is.

Years later, as I was traveling overland through India and saw the Kama Sutra statues that adorn nearly every temple there, I realized that in comparison, even porno itself is quite innocent. By then I was 45 years old.

# As Long as You've Got Some Cheese

Zerrin Koç

*Translated by Alvin Parmar*

We make acquaintances by coincidence and friends with time. Like it was with Chantelle.

When connoisseurs of conversations over drinks happen to be in Ankara, it is customary for them to end up in Sakarya Street. It was sheer coincidence that we found ourselves sitting at the same table as Chantelle in this narrow street that smells of aniseed and fried fish, lined on both sides with dicey-looking *meyhane meze* bars. I did not live in Ankara, nor did she, nor did dear Aysun. It was a mild June afternoon twenty-one years ago. Time has not always been as brazenly restless as it is today. It used to show more respect. It would dawdle more. (Or at least, that is it wants us to think so we can have fond memories of it.)

The three of us had come from Istanbul unbeknownst to each other and each for different reasons. I do not remember the details now, but Aysun had somehow managed to contact me. She said she was starting radiation therapy in Hacettepe and she would be done round about five o'clock, but I went earlier. We made our way to Sakarya Street arm in arm, laughing and joking with the joy of seeing each other, as if we were coming out of the cinema not the hospital. (Youth never gives up hope.) I do not know what I was wearing that day, but I have never forgotten Aysun's multicolored floral trousers.

On the way, she told me about a French friend of hers and said that she had called her too and that she might join us. I was only half listening, if I am honest. So much so that I did not even remember her name. I guess we each had a different June in our head. The place was almost empty when we sat down. We were already pretty deep in conversation when the evening drinkers started turning up in dribs and drabs. A group of six or seven foreigners suddenly appeared right next to us. Aysun only introduced one of them, Chantelle, to me. She did not know the others. They had come from a seminar the French Ministry of Education had organized through their embassy for their teachers serving in Turkey. All I recall about Chantelle from that evening was her very close-cropped black hair, her almond-shaped green eyes that seemed to have an aloof smile and her tiny face.

1976. A gloomy Paris morning with silver-white clouds hanging very low in the sky; the October rain was on its way. A dainty young girl in her twenties was getting ready to go out. When she looked in the mirror in her room, which was covered on all four walls with posters, instead of her own face, she saw kaleidoscopic reflections of Che Guevara, Fidel Castro, Stokely Carmichael, Martin Luther King and Alexander Dubček bouncing off the mirror from the walls. The door was emblazoned from top to bottom with the now fading words "Peace, Liberty, Equality, Fraternity". She closed it on the faces and set off for the School of Fine Arts.

1976. The wind was just starting to pick up in the mild October night; it was coming in from the sea. A little after midnight, a young woman was giving birth into the midst of the disorder in Anatolia, still raging on in the throes of civil strife, into a republic that was being dragged towards no one knew where.

1981. The dainty young girl with black hair and almond-shaped eyes was about to graduate with good marks from the School of Fine Arts. She got to know a young man from Istanbul called Harun who was studying at the same university and she set sail for love.

1981. As the far-reaching effects of the fascist coup in Turkey continued apace, the young woman was growing up together with her child. Feeling there was something wrong about *just being* a mother, she believed she had to do something. *Just being* was an incomplete, addictive feeling. She was looking for a form of rebellion where she could make her voice heard, where she could express herself.

"Aysun said you write poetry. I can't read Turkish. But I want to read your poems once I've learned." Chantelle, in her accented Turkish, told us a little about herself that evening. In four or five sentences, she said that as well as teaching art in a French high school, she did ceramics and sculpture in her own studio. And out of politeness, in return for the interest she took in my poetry, I told her I would like to see her work. But she did not promise out of politeness to send me an invitation to the exhibitions she would be having. That was the extent of the conversation between us that night.

After I came back to Istanbul, I did not see her for quite some time. To be honest, I never really thought about her. Then one day when Aysun said that she wanted to include her in our group, I remembered. At first, she did not join us very often and she would not say very much. We left her to her own devices. Actually, we were all leaving ourselves to our own devices without feeling the need to shelter behind our identities, without masks, without prejudice. The reason we would get together was so we could behave how we wanted to, let our hair down and get away from the problems of everyday life, even if it was only for four or five hours.

Chantelle did not let herself go until she had fully understood this spirit and made it her own. As time went on, she started joining us more often and she would bring her camera with her now and then to take our photos. We could see that she was getting more and more used to us and starting to trust us.

She would cook French food and invite us over. She would play us French songs she had listened to and fallen in love with when she was young and translate some of the words into Turkish. But, as someone whose mind is always cloudy, it took me a very long time to notice the natural grace in her movements and the depth in her limpid eyes. With her small, delicate smile perched on the edge of her lips, it looked as though she was listening to a rhapsodic melody. When I first noticed the calm expression on her face, like the languor of sleep, I was seized with a feeling of endlessness; she seemed to be looking in from outside of time. Our eyes would meet every so often and I sensed she had something she wanted to say. She knew me very well; she was looking at me as if she could read what was going through my mind and agreed with me. Maybe it was strange, but I did not feel at all uncomfortable. The interesting thing about it was that I had the feeling that if there was anyone who could understand me, then it was Chantelle. I had the sense that in me was the other half of all sorts of feelings that were left incomplete in her glances. You cannot explain the things you just know. That is just how it is...

Which wind had brought her to Istanbul? Was she not thinking of returning to Paris, a city that so many people are dying to move to? Did she not miss her country? I asked one night when we were sitting together.

She said that Marmaris was the first place she saw when she came to Turkey in the mid-Eighties after marrying Harun. She was very surprised when she stepped off the boat and right into some mud one hot summer's day. "My flip-flops and my feet got filthy." It was on this tour that she got to know Aysun and her husband. They journeyed northwards, touring historical places along the Aegean coast. She laughed when she was telling me that when they glided through the Dardanelles and into the Sea of Marmara, she was still a starry-eyed foreigner who had come to meet her husband's family and see where the man she was in love with had been born and raised. Then the inevitable happened the moment she set eyes on the Istanbul skyline on board the ship that had set its course for Karaköy harbor: "I was bewitched."

She was one of those people who fall in love with Istanbul at first sight. The plans she and her husband had made, the dreams they had had in Paris, all foundered in the Marmara. As they were approaching the end of their one-month holiday, they got into a bitter argument when she said she did not want to go back. Harun had absolutely no intention of staying in Turkey permanently; as far as he was concerned, the idea of living in Istanbul was completely ludicrous. It was a city that he would only visit on holiday, and then only for a short time, only to see his family.

He accused her of having succumbed to a passing Oriental phantasy. She should pull herself together right away because she was not a Pierre Loti. The Istanbul that Loti and other westerners who thought like him had created in their heads had been buried together with them. Their marriage took quite a battering because of the fight that broke out when he told her to prepare to go back right away. Chantelle, believing that everything would heal with time, started making different preparations. After she had her first child and moved to Istanbul, she never went back.

Paris was a city she went to on holiday or when she had a specific reason to go there.

Even though his plans had been turned on their head and his dreams shattered, for one year, Harun still hoped that she would agree to return to Paris. Chantelle did not know anyone in Turkey. She did not speak enough of the language. And she was not the sort of person who could form relationships easily. And even if she did, she was incapable of nurturing and growing a relationship. She had no idea about everyday life in Istanbul—how to deal with things and people. On top of that, she was very absentminded and forgetful.

When her enthusiasm wore off and she was confronted with reality, she would want to return to Paris. He hoped that it would not be long in coming because each day he was away worked against him in terms of business contacts he had made. But Chantelle had absolutely no intention of reversing her decision. She said that she had more or less guessed what difficulties she would meet and taken them into account.

If I am honest, I could not really understand where or what in this city she had fallen passionately enough in love with to put her marriage at risk. She thought for a moment and smiled; she continued in a voice that was calm, just like the expression on her face.

She was just finishing high school when the crowds filling the squares of Paris had enflamed the masses with their fiery belief and their burning anger. "We were going to make society honest by liberating it and changing the world. We started out boldly, rapturously, drastically. It didn't work. We couldn't see it through." It was at that time she left her family, who had deceived her with lies about the war, and a while later, while leaving the communal disappointment on the streets of Paris, she consigned De Gaulle to history too. "I was a living, breathing part of that universal dream." She started looking for herself in the void she fell into after she'd had this dream stolen from her; she met other people who were looking for themselves in the same void and had smoky, shadowy relationships. She drifted along with the currents and was scattered in the storms until she married Harun and came to Istanbul. "A vagabond life," she said, "an aimless, idling, vagabond life…"

Istanbul, according to Chantelle, was a magical storybook whose spell continued after you read it, where everyone created and wrote their own dreams. She could become part of this book on a page where she would make a fair copy of herself; she could write dreams that had been untouched by any hand. This strong belief, this unbearable desire she felt was itself the magic. Like every fairytale, there was something irresistibly attractive in its inconsistency, its confusion, its illogicalities that strained the human mind. The moment she said that if she had a magic wand, she would not be able to bring herself to wave it and put Istanbul in order, I saw her Istanbul in her eyes. It was a passionate double green.

By the time their second child was born, Harun had lost all hope of ever going back to Paris. Even though he had no doubt that his thoughts about his wife had been correct, he had been proved wrong. Chantelle was becoming more attached to Istanbul each day. By trying to act his part as a man with a sense of responsibility, he had upset the balance; he had got Chantelle used to taking the easy way out.

He fell into a quick tempo both at home and at work, and succumbed to a different kind of tiredness. When it all became too much and he felt the world was closing in, he would criticize his wife; he would accuse her of not giving a damn, of not being helpful. But each time Chantelle would give the same reply: "You organize everything.

You don't leave anything for me to do. You don't give me the chance. Because you don't trust me."

This could not have been the only problem blocking up their relationship. They could have gotten through it if it was. "Yes," she said, "It wasn't the only thing, but in the river of time, everything mingles together and becomes interrelated as it flows. He didn't find me attractive anymore. He didn't want to touch me or make love. It was Harun who was the foreigner."

It is exactly five years since this conversation. (Time has definitely taken the bit between its teeth and started to run.) In the meantime, we had started doing more things together. There were even more things we shared. We would go to the cinema, the theater, concerts; we would never miss any of Chantelle's exhibitions. We would coordinate very quickly on our difficult days; with a phone call we would find ourselves either at the hospital or sometimes in a mosque courtyard. "Like marriage vows," Chantelle used to say, "for better or worse, in sickness and in health." We would laugh.

She called me the other day. To be honest, I was surprised when she said she wanted to meet. It was the first time she was doing something like that: she was taking the initiative; she wanted to meet face to face. She was also part of a group exhibition the next day. She said we could meet there. I immediately cancelled what I had been thinking of doing and told her I was waiting for her at home that evening. And I did not forget to add that I did not have any food. "As long as you've got some cheese," she said.

She came exactly when she said she would, at half past seven that evening. She thrust a bottle of wine into my hand as soon as she was inside. While she was taking off her coat, her hat, her gloves, she said the traffic had been unbelievable. Was she still not thinking of using her magic wand? She laughed.

Apparently she was not. When she went through to the living room and sat down at the table, I brought the corkscrew over. She took it from me. "You can't do it properly," she said. "You make the cork disintegrate. If you do that around French people, they'll make fun of you mercilessly." And around her? "I'm not one of them." In which sense, I wonder. Not one of the French who would make fun of me or not one of the French full stop? I did not ask.

Our conversation lasted until five in the morning. She talked about her childhood, the religious school that she was forced to go to when she was ten after her mother remarried, and the two terrible years she spent there. "She kept me there for two years, even though I begged her not to. I suffered so much. I didn't forgive her for years." She talked about her father, her brothers and sisters. The things she was telling me did not strike me as particularly unfamiliar. Like two heroes roaming through the same story, our paths kept crossing all the time. My instincts had not let me down. We were speaking in the shared language of our suffering; we finished off each other's half-finished words. Jarred feelings: half with her, the other half with me.

When she said she had forgiven the past and did not think about it anymore, I was out of the story. To forgive and forget was more than I could manage. She said it was not difficult. "You've really got to believe that death won't only knock on other people's doors. Then the past no longer has any importance." She had misunderstood. I had no intention of biting the hand of the past that brought me into existence by feeding me bitter mouthfuls. I just smiled.

The friendship that we had left to time developed and grew even more as the hours went by. With the intensity of the belief that we would not regret it afterwards, we shared our secrets. Secrets that we avoided confessing even to ourselves, that we avoided confronting...

Did she want to have a hot drink? Tea, Turkish coffee, instant coffee? She thought for a moment. "Another glass of wine if there's any left," she said. There was some. After taking a mouthful from her refilled glass, it was time for the recent past. She was saying she had forgiven it and she did not think about it, but if you ask me, it was just words. Wanting is one thing; doing is another. I kept my thoughts to myself. She told me about the morning Harun left saying there was someone else in his life. Was that when she first found out there was another woman? She said she had felt it. "He'd humiliate me and insult me." In what way? "He'd say I was a run-of-the-mill French woman, petty bourgeois, a little civil servant, with simple pleasures and small dreams."

I could not believe my ears. Was it really Harun who had said all that? "His father was a doctor," she said. "He had a lot of respect for the medical profession." That is all well and good, but what has it got to do with anything? She had found out during the fight they had that morning that his lover Gülden was a young doctor. "I personally didn't care one way or the other what she did, but it was important for Harun." She had felt so offended, so wounded, so deeply humiliated that she had wanted to take a handful of pills and die. None of us knew these details. "I realized once more that I had been right to always trust you. You helped so much without knowing it!"

Chantelle was a prolific artist who had grown up in the artistic center of Europe and who did ceramics and sculpture as well as teaching. The things she liked could not be simple; her thoughts could not be small. The sorrow that settled in her pupils when I mentioned this extended all the way to her smile. "I'm small because I sabotaged his dreams for the sake of creating my own," she said. "I'm simple because I preferred

Istanbul over Paris."

She said it was all water under the bridge as she sighed and leaned back. "Harun respects me now; he respects me a lot. We often meet up and share our troubles. We're better now than we were able to be when we were married. He's still the person who helps me out the most. I've kept his name. He's never given up on his responsibilities towards us." What could I say? Harun was obviously one of those people who prefers the uphill path. I remembered a French saying while she was telling me that: If you want to make two people enemies, make them live in the same house. She said she had not heard it before. "It might have come in handy if I'd heard it earlier." Her smile, like her voice, was sardonic. Her elder son was about to finish university. The younger one was getting ready to go to university. Harun and Gülden got married two years ago. But what about Chantelle? What was keeping her here? Was she still not thinking of going back? Her answer was a definite no. "Every city has a mirror," she said. "I saw myself in Istanbul's mirror as that ship was approaching Karaköy twenty-four years ago. I was a ghost in Paris; I became real here. Would you have gone back if you'd been in my place?" Bless you, Chantelle. I emigrated from the past. And if I was going to go back, I would go back via the past.

She said she wanted to raise her glass to us, "Because you made my most difficult times easier, because you're in my life..." She drained the wine she had left. She opened her bag. She took out a medium-sized yellow envelope. She had brought an invitation and the exhibition catalog. I glanced at the main title: *Five women Five stories.* Opening the page about her, she asked me to read out loud the introductory article she had written herself. She had called her series of works "The Women's Movement". "Ignore the mistakes in my writing. I can't write as well as I speak." I read: "In the behaviors of my Turkish friends, I have always seen the way they laugh, the way they comb their hair and their other gestures as enchanting, as the acme of femininity. As for me, some expressions and movements—neither French nor Turkish— have always struck me. Every country's culture still has gestures that are specific to it, and behaviors—fortunately—have not yet (!) become global. In this series, I wanted to portray the originality of my Turkish friends' femininity via their movements. I dedicate it to them. Chantelle Marie Atakan."

And I dedicate this story to you, dear Chantelle. (And if I have made any slips of the tongue, you ignore them too.)

# Delusions in the Heart of a Giant

Yasemin Yazıcı

*Translated by Mark David Wyers*

Utrecht, a city in the center of the country; the heart of the Dutch, their first settlement, their homeland. Cemal wasn't born there. But the longer he lived in this city, the first he had seen in Europe, the more he came to like it. At every opportunity, he would lose himself in the city's streets, overtaken by an uncanny feeling of happiness. He wandered the neighborhoods, markets, lanes and canal bridges which were nothing like those in his hometown in Anatolia, but sometimes when he came face-to-face with the seemingly flat existence of the Dutch, he would plummet into the depths of an emptiness he carried within and be driven from thought to thought by strange winds.

He had borrowed a bicycle from his cousin. It was one of those old black bicycles that everyone used. The rims were a little corroded, the leather seat worn out. But Cemal really enjoyed riding. When he rode, he was uplifted by a sense of freedom that was beyond flight. He was the black-browed, dark-eyed, olive-skinned son of a large, poor family who had migrated from Anatolia. Like every newcomer, as he tried to adjust to this small European city, he wanted to throw off that sense of foreignness that seeped into every aspect of his life.

At times, he was like a small child that stood facing a fairytale giant. He wanted to not fear the giant, he wanted to touch it, but an instinctive dread held him back and his courage failed him.

He had found a temporary job in one of the covered shopping areas that opened onto the Jaarbeurs train station. He was in charge of cleaning up, but it was just interim work because they wouldn't hire him full-time. One of the employees had gone on vacation, and he was just filling in. In any case, he was going to start university in the fall. He had passed a two-year language course with good marks. In his family, he was the star child. There are those large families in which one or two children shine, leaving the others behind, and the others toil with all their might so that at least one of them will succeed, giving up a part of their lives along the way. Cemal was one of those outstanding children and made his family proud. Perhaps he was lucky, but most of the time, rather than making him happy, this left him with a sense of bitterness. It was as though his life was made up of the hopes of his family and didn't completely belong to him.

When he went outside after his shift, the sun gleamed in his eyes. It was rare weather. The sun, as though kidnapped from the south, glimmered over the city, spilling warm light into every corner. Cemal grumbled to himself, "After this heat, surely it's going to rain." Taking side streets, he headed towards the edge of the canal where his bicycle was locked up.

Eleven o'clock and the sun was bathing the city in light.

He unlocked his bicycle. Leaving the crowded market behind, he turned onto a random street. As the day warmed up, the locals stripped down and enjoyed the weather. Young women in miniskirts and shorts quickly pedaled their bicycles, bustling from one place to another. As these blond muses came and went, Cemal felt more elated. His confidence rose and he whistled as he assumed a new identity in a new world. He swerved from left to right as a swarm of bicycle bells chimed behind him, and he generously made way for these intrepid cyclists.

Passing the sculpture of Oranje, the nation's founder, he continued straight down the road. Then he took a break on one of the benches among the large trees of the Maliebaan. He lit a cigarette. For a while, he sat and rested in the cool shade of the trees. Just across the way, trucks were being unloaded for a traveling amusement park. He sat for a while and watched the workers; then he flicked his cigarette butt on the ground and stamped it out. Getting back on his bicycle, he followed the cyclist signs painted on the street which led to the city's outskirts. An elderly couple silently passed him and sped ahead in single file. There were packages of food and drinks in the baskets of their bicycles. Cemal followed behind. He watched them move into the distance and was lost in thought, riding aimlessly.

"Today is Wednesday," he thought. "On Wednesday, there is a market in Vredenburg." Suddenly the image of the girl from whom he bought pastries and bread appeared in his mind's eye. The girl had traveled to the seaside of Turkey, which Cemal had never seen, and said that she had really liked the people there. The people, she said, were so warm-hearted and hospitable. Saying this, she gave him a free cookie. He had been living in Holland for two years, and that was the first time anyone had ever offered him anything. At that moment, he was so pleased that he finally felt he was at home in this country. Even if it was fleeting, that refreshing feeling of belonging filled him with a sense of comfort. Whenever despair unexpectedly overwhelmed him, he would replay that scene in his mind, just like someone in a desert dying of thirst dreams of water.

On Wednesdays, most of the residents of Utrecht go to the market in Vredenburg. That day, it was also crowded. As he was moving through the crowd to get some bread, the girl working at the stand suddenly asked:

"Where are you from?"

By this time, Cemal spoke Dutch quite well. With a shy smile, he answered "Turkey". The girl laughed cheerfully, and showing off her tan, said, "I was there last week, it was so much fun. Your country is wonderful! Such friendly people."

He listened to her raptly, as though he were taking in the words of those beautiful women who appear topless on the back pages of popular Turkish newspapers. With an innocent smile she passed him a butter cookie in a gloved hand, along with the bread she had put in a bag.

"This is on me!"

It was like the girl had run into an old Dutch friend; she offered the cookie with a sincerity born of forty years of friendship. Cemal accepted the cookie, and gingerly placed it into the bag.

"*Tot ziens,*" the girl said goodbye, and, like an image in a mirror, with the same smile and the same emphasis, he answered, "Tot ziens."

As he moved through the crowd that day he felt more at ease. In fluent Dutch, he bought a fried fish sandwich and, sitting on an empty bench in the train station, began to eat. He was filled by a sense of tranquility that he had not felt for a long time. As he watched the families tugging along their luggage, the young men and women wearing backpacks, and the women walking alone pulling wheeled suitcases, he ate his lunch slowly, relishing each bite. As he ate, he noticed that the Kurdish, Turkish and Moroccan workers were cleaning the station. Cemal felt an affinity with them that no Dutch person could understand. Later, as he threw away the sandwich paper, he was flooded with a sense of belonging. Filled with emotions that he could not put into words or even consciously formulate, he was rapturous as he ate the cookie, which he washed down with a fruit-yogurt drink he bought from a kiosk.

While he was lost in that emotional reverie, the elderly couple cycling ahead of him had disappeared from sight. There was a fork in the road. He slowed down, and putting one foot down, stopped. Then he began pedaling again, and for no reason at all, took the road to the left. "How could I get lost in such a small town?" he thought. He proceeded down the narrow dirt path, which was bordered by tightly grouped rows of trees.

It was the first week of June, and the northerners were desperate not to miss this stolen day of southern sunshine. First he heard the voices and laughter of children from behind the trees. He listened to their joyful cries for a while. Getting off his bicycle, he pushed it by the handlebars over the grass in the direction of the voices. Among the trees, an area appeared which seemed newly built, a kind of natural park. Water from a fountain flowed down a narrow canal that snaked through the grass to a nearby pond. Shouting with delight, the children chased their toy boats and ducks that floated down the canal, and when they arrived at the pond, they brought them back up to the top. Some of the children played in the sand at the shore of the pond and waded into the water, and some of them crossed a half-submerged bridge in daring journeys of the imagination. Light-skinned women who had come alone or with their friends reclined under the sun and chatted, read or played with the children. Few men had come for the lunch break. Those who were there were either eating sandwiches or reading the newspaper.

Cemal leaned his bicycle against the trunk of a young tree and sat in the moist grass of the tree's narrow shadow. Spring feelings welled up inside of him. He looked at the clusters of clouds in the sky, and closed his eyes. As he listened to the shouting of the children, suddenly his mind skipped to the pale, dusty, bitter memories of his own childhood and friends, and the joy in his heart withered. Wanting to distance himself from those old memories, he opened his eyes. A group of blond children were filling their buckets at the fountain and emptying them into the pond, racing across the grass. Cemal watched them for a while. The children, both boys and girls, were naked. The mothers had stripped down to their bikinis, their bodies accustomed to nature, a little plump, with a little cellulite, pale-skinned; they were beautiful mothers.

Cemal thought, "Like the paintings from the old days." The women resembled those he had seen in the Renaissance paintings at the National Museum in Amsterdam; it was as if those plump, young, naked women were picnicking with winged cherubs at the waterside. What he was seeing was just a new version of an old painting. Nudity was not sexuality, it was spirituality. The inside pulsing outward. Even if Cemal could not put it into words in such detail, he could feel that knowledge in his heart.

The sky was an intense blue and the clouds drifted low overhead. The grass, free of insects, was laid out like a carpet. He took off his shirt and pressed his skin to the cool of the grass. A chill ran through him. He felt himself shrouded in the innocence of nakedness. Naked and free of sin. But again, for a reason he couldn't understand, a pained feeling unsettled him. He closed his eyes. With the sound of flowing water and the shouting of children ringing in his ears, he fell into dreams.

It felt like for two years he had been rushing between school and work and had not even experienced the city. Now, the door was ajar, and the sounds coming from within had become words that he could finally understand. He was looking for a place where he could forget his foreignness. Any place.

Time passed, and Cemal was about to awake from the dreams of his daytime nap. A sudden chill ran through him and he opened his eyes. The sun had vanished and the clouds had darkened. As he scrambled up and pulled on his shirt, he realized that he was tired but had somehow overlooked his fatigue. His body, along with his dreams, had fallen into a thick stupor. He glanced around.

When had the women and children left?

There was just one woman and her son across the way. The woman was absent-mindedly writing something in a notebook. Her son, probably around five years old, was chasing his toy duck as it floated down the chilly water.

The woman suddenly snapped out of her reverie as if she heard a warning shot, and looked around; Cemal and the woman came eye to eye. The woman appeared concerned at the fact that all of the other picnickers had left, which she just now noticed.

She hurriedly began to pack her bag and to call out to her son. Cemal paused. A sense of guilt clung to him. He didn't know what to do. He felt guilty that she was packing up quickly and yelling for her son, who wasn't listening to her.

Her son was jumping in the water. "A little longer, a little longer!" he pleaded. The woman's unease had turned into panic; she was now shouting at her son in sharp tones.

At that moment, Cemal felt like a giant who had transformed that new age Renaissance painting into a nightmare. A thick melancholy churned inside him. This fairytale giant was actually good-hearted, but nobody understood this because of his terrifying appearance.

The woman rapidly gathered her things, scooped up the toys her son had spread around, and stuffed them into the basket of her bicycle. Then she ran and picked up her son, and hurriedly changed his clothes. The child had begun to cry.

From afar, Cemal called out to her, his voice heavy with that giant's gloom that had gathered within him, "Please, don't be afraid."

The woman was seating her son on the bicycle. It seemed that she didn't understand what Cemal had said.

As he got on his bicycle, Cemal called out again:

"Please don't be afraid, I am leaving now"

Without saying a word, the woman looked at him. Hesitation in her eyes. Distress.

As Cemal rode, he turned and looked back for a moment. The woman had placed her son on the rear seat and was quickly riding the other way. Cemal was pedaling with all his might, panting, fleeing straight into the depths of the forest; he was now a strange-looking giant, and he rode with all the force of his massive broken heart. He was filled with a sadness that swelled within him. It rose up, wave after wave, drowning his spirit, choking him. Suddenly he saw the elderly woman and her husband. He was so surprised that he didn't hit the brakes. They careened into each other.

When the elderly woman's husband fell to the ground, she swerved to a stop. The old man's head was bleeding. Cemal stared at the flowing blood in astonishment. The woman's aged, pale blue eyes were filled with rage and contempt. With the despair of a giant, Cemal merely stood there. He was afraid to move, to inflict any more harm. With his remaining strength, he leaned down towards the man. He touched him. The body didn't move. He was dead. The woman was screaming, "Police, police!" There was no one around. The world was filled with desolation. Unaware of what he was doing, he moved towards the woman.

"Dirty foreigner!" she screamed. "Dirty foreigner!"

Cemal felt himself taking on that sense of guilt. In fact, what he wanted to do was go back, to embrace those dreams that the bright daytime sun had granted him. Then he noticed that he had picked up the bicycle pump and cracked the woman over the head with it. But it was against his will, like someone else inside of him had taken over and was guiding his movements. The woman crumpled to the ground in a bloody heap. He looked at the pump in his hand; it was covered in blood.

"Look, he's coming around!"

Cautiously, he opened his eyes. The elderly couple was by his side. Their voices were inflected with concern.

"Are you okay? Do you want to go to the hospital?"

"No," Cemal said. His voice was like a child's when awoken from a bad dream, full of surprise, dread and joy.

"Nothing hurts… I must have fainted. But what about you, are you okay?"

The matching blue eyes of the couple glinted with humor.

"We are fine. In fact, what happened is that you crashed into a tree. Are you sure you are okay?"

Cemal's head began to clear. He got up and picked up his bicycle.

"I… I was afraid that I had crashed into you," he said, looking into their faces with disbelief.

As the elderly couple got back onto their bicycles, they smiled.

"Ah, that's youth. If we had fallen like that, we couldn't have gotten back up as easily as you," the man said.

Together, the man and woman crossed the forest path and rode up to the street. Cemal was reeling. Raindrops had begun to spatter down.

As they turned down a lane, the elderly couple waved and said:

"*Goedendag*!"

"Goedendag!"

As Cemal rode along the street, he was soaked by the sudden rain and shivered. But somehow that shiver felt good. "Tomorrow is Wednesday," he thought. "I'll go to the market and do some shopping. Maybe the girl who sells bread will give me another cookie."

# Laptop

Feride Çiçekoğlu

*Translated by Alvin Parmar*

When you sat down directly opposite me, our eyes almost met.

But on this journey, I'd made my mind up to obey that rule common both to subway systems and prisons and not make eye contact.

I can't remember which stop you got on at. I'm following the dark blue Piccadilly Line on the London Underground map, starting from Heathrow Airport: Hatton Cross, Hounslow West, Hounslow Central, Hounslow East, Osterley... Which one was it? It must be one of the Hounslows. I don't know.

Was there only one empty seat when you got on, or did you choose to sit across from me? I'd like to think you chose to sit there, but after wracking my brains, I seem to think there weren't any other empty seats. We were among the millions of people who had got out of the millions of planes, with our coats, our umbrellas and our suitcases. It was the last empty seat I think, the one you sat in, but maybe you were pleased because it was still empty. Otherwise, why would our eyes have almost met?

Arriving at Heathrow this time, my luggage, the way I walked, but most of all the way I kept my chin up so I had to look down on everyone meant that no one could touch me, not even in the visa queue. And my wheeled suitcase, with its telescopic handle that locks with a nifty click when extended, and which obediently follows me, is a Carlton, a British brand. It has a bright pink British Council sticker on it too. So add that to my withering glance, and the visa official, far from asking questions, is reduced to making apologies. No more bags with handles that snap in half in the airport after you've bought some books. And no more looking into people's eyes and smiling. It's that easy! Your eyes show what level you're on. If you're on top, then everything's okay.

But I hate people who don't look you in the eye. And there are different ways of not doing it. Looking away, looking at your feet, blinking, fixing your eyes on somewhere out in the distance... Looking someone in the eye is about courage. Take a look if you think you're brave enough. Then you'll find out for yourself the rule about having to sneer into the eyes of visa officials. If your humanity gets the better of you, though, don't look. But what about on the Underground?

Only "foreigners" make eye contact on the Underground. I've made up my mind not to be a foreigner this time. You're obviously the same. Still, the sort of electricity there is between us means that we would have looked at each other, if only fleetingly, if we hadn't already decided not to. It hangs in the air halfway between us as the train lurches.

I proceed to look attentively over your left shoulder and out the window. A matte black cable runs past, shifting height from time to time. The blackness of your skin, though, is shiny and soft. You've got prominent cheekbones and an aquiline nose. If I could see you from the side, I can tell your profile would remind me of a pharaoh's. You're too dark for the Nile Delta. Too light for the Upper Nile. You must be Nubian, a descendant of Nefertiti.

And you're looking over my right shoulder, through the window behind me and outside. My hand is about to straighten my hair automatically, but I stop it halfway and straighten my glasses needlessly instead. I mean, what would be the point of me straightening out my hair; that's how it is.

I shift my eyes to the left, passing over your forehead, and stare fixedly at the same point outside, so as not to give myself away. Your forehead is broad and prominent, so my journey along your hairline takes quite a long time. Because I know I won't be able to escape if my glance catches on your hair or your lips, I'm just about to glide my eyes from your forehead and focus this time over your right shoulder and then outside, when I notice the person sitting on your right.

His head only comes up to your shoulder. Is it because he's sitting next to you that he seems so bewildered and pathetic, or is he really like that? I can't decide. His complexion is sallow like he's spent his whole life out of the sun, always traveling in the Underground instead. His sparse, indecisive hair, which looks like it'll never be clean no matter what it's washed with, is combed in a side part. Acne. He must be in his twenties, practically half your, or rather our, age. It's no problem for me to look at his eyes, minified as they are behind his thick glasses, because they're earnestly glued to the keyboard of his laptop. He's trying to type something with movements that appear awkward even to my untrained eye. He's wearing a suit that drowns him and a patterned wide tie. Multicolored African animals. Bright orange giraffes, stripy zebras, huge rhinos, then giraffes again.

We lurch to a halt. I notice I've forgotten to keep track of which station I'm getting out at ever since you got on. We're still far in the west of London. No need to panic. The doors open; one person gets out; a crowd of people get on. The area by the doors is packed. A family with two children. On the strap hanging from the woman's neck, her little baby who she clasps to her breast. It can't be more than a month old. And a three- or four-year-old boy clinging to his father's hand. The man's medium height and chubby; the woman's the same. There's something about them that doesn't resemble you, like they're not descended from the same pharaonic line.

The woman clings to the pole next to the laptop man and tries to keep her balance. Her right hand's on her little one's back. She's gently patting it and soothing it. We lurch off again. The little one doesn't care and must be used to it.

The laptop man is agitated, fidgeting. Then I notice what's written above him: "Priority seat for people who are disabled, pregnant or less able to stand." Pretending not to know what to do with his laptop, he looks helplessly first at the woman with the child, and then, without giving him the chance to look at you, you get up. The woman comes and sits in your seat. No one looks at anyone; no one says a single word. No please, no thank you, no sorry I couldn't get up, nothing.

You're completely out of my field of vision, so I can only sense you standing in the area by the doors. Partly because he's pushed you away from me entirely, I proceed to stare down the laptop man, angrily and recklessly. He definitely has a difficult mother. A mother who doesn't yell twice that dinner's ready. Probably an only child too. His mother will have spoken with his teachers every week from primary school until the end of university. "What? Literature? Are you out of your mind?" And the moment he heard her footsteps, he'd have hidden the poetry he wrote in secret. It would have been decided that he'd study business management. He's anxious like his mother's going to get on at the next station and scold him if he's not working. The more he feels me staring straight at him, the more awkward he becomes. Serves him right! A computer's unpleasant enough in an office or on a desk. But on your lap like that, and in the Underground of all places. Who knows what he's struggling to write, with his stubby fingers getting ever clumsier. They couldn't play the piano or paint a picture; they're indecisive, weak.

I suddenly wonder what your hands are like. I try to figure out where you are first of all, so as not to appear to be looking for you. The furthest you'll be is where the woman you gave your seat to was standing. She's sitting directly opposite me now, staring off into space. She doesn't see the black cable flowing past the window, me, the Underground map to the top left of my head, or the restaurant, condom and nappy ads that follow one after the other above me. Her dress is yellow with black checks. Her hand's on her baby's back.

Hands... Your hands? I keep my eyes at the level of the woman and the laptop man's head and find the pole she was holding a short while ago. A little higher, and there's your hand. You've gripped the pole nicely. Your fingers are long. You don't play the saxophone by any chance, do you? There's jazz in your fingertips. It's obvious, whatever you touch turns to jazz. And you've got a ring on your little finger, with a blue stone. African, not wannabe African like the animals on the tie.

Orange giraffes, a huge rhino... We lurch to a halt.

The woman gets up indifferently and walks to the door. They get out as a family. Your seat's empty. Movement at the edge of my right eye's field of vision. Between people sitting facing each other, someone who's standing somewhere he shouldn't be, a man, Eastern European from the language he's speaking with the people next to him, climbs over the suitcases and makes a move that reveals his intention to get to your seat. Seizing the opportunity, I look first at him, then at you. A little longer at you.

As you and the man face each other, you pause for a moment. You offer him the seat with a subtle movement of your eyebrows and a polite gesture of your hand. Clever. The seat's yours, but you relinquish it. The man understands. He understands and changes his mind. He puts his leg, which he was about to stretch over a suitcase, back in the stable position it was in just before.

And there you are again directly opposite me.

I give up on my decision not to make eye contact. This time I'm determined to catch the eye contact you missed by a hair's breadth the first time you sat down. Just as I'm looking at the point where I know I'll find your eye…

"If I didn't have to solve this, I'd have got up…"

He really knew how to pick his moment for an apology. What happened to not talking to anyone you don't know and not making eye contact with anyone on the Underground? He did it just to spite me, I know he did. You'll put him in his place and then make it to our eye date. Where was I supposed to be getting off? Where are we now? Come on, before one of us gets off…

"It doesn't matter!" you laugh. Not to me, but to the idiot next to you. Your teeth are pure white; your voice has a lilt to it that reveals the rhythm of your body. Just like I thought it would. Anyway, you've spent enough time on the person next to you now.

But he won't leave you alone. "There's something wrong with the program," he says, whining about his laptop. I'm expecting you to shut him up once and for all by saying, "What do you expect if you're typing on the Underground?" What work could possibly be so urgent? His sole intention is to show off his laptop and hide behind it. You'll manage to make a fool of him. And you'll do it so subtly that he won't even realize you're mocking him. Once he's gone back to what he's doing, we'll share the joke, eye to eye. But come on!

"That's a nice machine," you say.

"Nooo," he says modestly. "It's an old model, pretty rubbish really."

Orange giraffes...

We've stopped. Should I get off? Where are we?

"How much would you pay for one like that?"

Black and white zebras...

I don't catch the price as we lurch off again, but from your joy, they're obviously dirt cheap.

"Really?" you say interestedly.

"Of course," he says, with a new self-assured decisiveness in his voice.

"Where can you get them from?"

"Near Oxford Street. I can show you if you've got a map."

You take out your map from your inside jacket pocket. In London, everyone has a map. Especially foreigners. I check mine's still in the front compartment of my bag; it is. Good. How many stations until I have to get off?

You and the laptop man stroll down Oxford Street on the map, together. "Ha, there it is, this corner," he says. "I'll mark it for you if you've got a pen."

You don't have one. He does. Of course. Actually, it's inside the briefcase underneath his laptop. So be it. He passes his laptop over to you, takes out his pen and puts a mark on your map. He's just about to put it back in his case again when he changes his mind and puts it in his inside pocket instead. He sets the laptop back on top of the case. You say thank you, fold up your map and put it in your inside jacket pocket. Like you're in a hurry.

"Bye," you say. Not to me, to him.

We lurch to a halt as you're getting up from your seat. We've reached Acton Town. You get off. You must be going to change for one of the lines going north. In the station, you look around for a moment as if you don't know what direction you're going in. The doors close. We lurch off.

A huge rhino...

Giraffes...

# Neverending

Selma Sancı

*Translated by Mark David Wyers*

It had been a difficult trip. They had left early, and her husband, as
though accompanying her merely out of a sense of duty, hadn't spoken
to her once on the bus, never taking his eyes off the road.

The impenetrable darkness of that cold morning was itself tire-
some. She felt disoriented in the airport, which swarmed with people.
In the restroom mirror, she observed her outdated overcoat, messy hair
and haggard face. Being there, among the women freshening up their
makeup, the shouting children and excited travelers, made her feel
even worse.

Finally, they boarded the plane to Switzerland. Pressing her coat
into her lap, she shrank into her aisle seat and watched the other passengers settle in. There was a bald man wearing glasses sitting in the
window seat in her row. After the plane took off, her husband, who
appeared not to have noticed him, set about speaking with the man,
talking about his job as a teacher, his novel, and how he wrote about his
village in the novel. Unable to resist, he invited the man to his public
reading, and even mentioned that they planned to visit some relatives
who were working in a town near Geneva. Behiye was petrified that
the word "prison" would slip out of his mouth as well.

The man never spoke. Occasionally he would turn, and with a dull expression, look at Kemal's black suit, his loosened tie, and the collar of his striped shirt, which was too large for his thin neck.

Behiye flipped through a magazine she had pulled from the pocket of the seat in front of her, but in her unease, didn't understand anything she read. Flight attendants pushed and pulled the food cart up the length of the aisle. There was the hum of chatter, and her ears rang. Her excitement rose, and fell. She didn't want to go anywhere.

She leaned her head against the headrest and began thinking. She imagined Serpil waiting on rows of tables draped in bright white tablecloths in a large restaurant. She tried not to think about how, after prison, she hadn't been able to stand for long on her feet. Apparently she was working in the kitchen. Maybe it was the friend who was a waitress who had found her a job in that town, a place which even travel agencies didn't know about. That's what the woman had said on the phone, in a manner of speaking. When she heard Serpil's name, she had a sudden desire to see her. She asked for the name of the restaurant and the address, syllable by syllable, and even wrote a letter. But then she changed her mind about sending it. She had always wanted to find a way to come; every thought that went through her mind returned to that.

The plane trembled, startling her. Allah, let this journey be over... Let me be able to see Serpil, to talk with her... Under the damp light of the shores of that lake, let it be as though my troubles have been washed away, she said to herself. As an announcement was being made, she opened her eyes. There was a grimy white luminescence visible through the window. Allah, you are great... save my child... help me, Allah, she whispered. A short while later, they disembarked, the man wearing glasses graciously helped them into a taxi, and half an hour later, they arrived at the desolate shores of the lake.

* * *

The weather was humid and the fog was thick as a blanket. Without talking, they walked through a stony, secluded area. Pointing to a stone bench, Kemal said, "Let's sit a little." His expression was glum; it was clear that he wanted to go back home.

They sat for a while, observing the setting around them. The road behind them, lined on both sides by bare trees, stretched emptily into the distance. Like a breeze from an open window, a coolness blew in from the lake. The excitement of going to a new place she had been imagining in all of its enchantment had vanished. Aside from the cold of the stone bench, she felt nothing else.

Behiye was hurt by her husband's glumness, and even this pain was too much for her. For years, it had been like this: manage the household, move from place to place, leave the shop, go to the market, cook, make sure the baby gets enough vegetables, the babysitter didn't give the baby any fruit, don't raise your voice, argue with the landlord, don't get upset…

She remembered that morning like it was yesterday: the old woman living downstairs had caught her at the entryway of the apartment building. She went on and on about how badly things were going, about how it was so important for the apartment building to be peaceful, about how she wasn't sure about those people who visited.

To shake off her thoughts, she suddenly stood up. She took two steps, and a deep breath. She looked at Kemal, sitting there with the suitcase by his feet and his shoulders slumped. He was looking at the ground, lost in thought. Why was he so lost in thought? It was just a talk. But still, she didn't bring up the issue of the book. She let the anger welling inside of her cool off. They decided that Kemal would go back. They slowly walked back to where the taxi had dropped them off. She shouldn't worry. He would be gone before evening.

* * *

As the taxi pulled away, a feeling of sadness overwhelmed her. She forced herself to think pleasant thoughts and plunged her hands deep into her coat pockets. First, she wanted to go to the lakeshore. She walked down the asphalt road parallel to the town square. Silence had enveloped the city. A few passengers waited at a small stone pier, a boat seemed to glide over the surface of the lake, the whiteness of the mountains glimmered in the distance, and a stately chateau with tall windows topped by arches, built in who knows which century, overlooked the foggy lake.

A tall woman walking a small dog walked past her, wearing a white plastic raincoat that hung to her feet. With one hand she held the leash tight, and the dog walked obediently beside her. The loneliness of the woman touched Behiye's heart. Women were lonely everywhere. Beneath the overcast sky, she was haunted by images of the past, and in the silence that accompanied the clouds, the small lake and the mountains rising up from the shore, she wondered how Serpil was doing. She was impatient to get to town and she began walking back.

That morning, the Kadıköy pier and in the distance, the European side of Istanbul had been shrouded in fog as well. She had disembarked at Haydarpaşa station and seen the missing persons poster on the exit door of the dimly lit corridor. She immediately stopped and then hastened away in fear, joining the crowd rushing down the stairs and leaping onto the ferry. For a while, thoughts of the landlord's insults at the apartment entryway floated through her mind, and it was as if all of the strength in her body drained out of her fingertips. She sat on the outer deck of the ferry, and from the corner of her eye observed the last passengers jump on board and the rope that the dockhand tossed from shore as it soared through the air. Throughout the trip, she kept seeing Serpil's face, smiling ever so slightly, imprisoned in a black square on the poster, and she recalled Serpil's timidity when they had lived together.

She quickened her pace, crossing the field and the straight, tree-lined road. She turned at the first intersection and headed up the main road which hummed with traffic. Stopping to catch her breath in front of a shop that had gloves and hats in its display window, she wanted to free herself, even if just a little, from the worry and unease she carried inside. She read the label attached to a pair of gloves, admired the color of another, and fell into a reverie looking at the bows stitched along the edges of a hat. It calmed her.

When she had gathered the courage to look around again, she saw a restaurant across the street, its windows slightly fogged. A jolt ran through her. Not aware of her own movements, she hastened her steps. Later, noting with surprise the state she was in, she slowed down. She tried to hold back her nervousness. Like a shadow, she walked down the street, the buildings embellished with plaster adornments, and as she walked, she recalled images of the day Serpil moved out, of her slow descent down the stairs with a large bag weighing down her shoulder; the hopelessness of leaving … averted glances … the tears she couldn't hold back.

All day at work she was out of breath, consumed, obsessed, and that evening she fought with her husband; a simple wave of a hand would have been enough to raze their lives to the ground. She was so young, so inexperienced. She hadn't noticed Serpil's anxiousness that day, and wasn't able to help shoulder her troubles. Where had she gone? Where could she go? With that large bag, she would be picked up right away. If she hadn't had a child, would she have just watched Serpil walk away? She didn't even care about the loans and her new shop. If only Serpil knew. If only Serpil knew that she couldn't have left her child, would she forgive her?

She was walking through the mist, trying to find a way to sort out the confusion in her mind. There were no car horns, no irritating noises. The only thing that they couldn't bring under control in this orderly town that ran like clockwork was the weather. She should admit that when she was on the way here, her dreams had unraveled and fallen away, and it became clear that the things she had wanted to say were useless. Now, she understood that pushing Serpil to work too hard had caused her health problems and that focusing just on work had driven her to loneliness. Their lives had been used up, and now here she was, hopeless, and Serpil was here too, all alone.

She came to the end of the street. She crossed and began quickly walking back. The broad sidewalk stretched before her. When she realized that she was approaching the restaurant, she slowed down. As she passed by the entrance, she hesitated and looked inside. It was off-season and the restaurant was quiet. A gray-haired couple sat by the window drinking coffee. Waitresses bustled in the large restaurant, looking busier than they needed to be. At a long table, a group of mostly elderly but well-groomed, ruddy women had gathered. With their grayish-blond hair, they resembled one another. They sat with dignified confidence, leaning back in their chairs. Perhaps it was a birthday party or a society meeting. Because they were forced to sit at the same table with people whose friendship they didn't seek, to talk about issues they weren't interested in, and because the only thing they shared was loneliness, they were forced to appear as friends. She lamented that her own bitter friendship with Serpil, which had brought her to this silent city and left her to roam its streets, was a thing of the past. What would happen if she could actually bring herself to go inside?

At another table, men wearing gray suits were sipping wine. Maybe they had come from Geneva, weekend customers. This small town was a place for people who enjoyed being far from the gaze of others and were fed up with popular tourist spots, a sequestered resting place for a handful of individuals. Here, there were none of the endless difficulties of people's lives in cities, with their annoyances and roaring traffic. There were no streets with concrete buildings that loomed above like cliffs as you walked between them.

An expressionless young man wearing a white jacket was standing at the large glass door of the restaurant. Was it the discomfort of being in a place with which she was not familiar? The fear that Serpil would suddenly appear in front of her? Or had some other fear taken hold? She didn't go inside. As she passed by the young man, she felt even more displaced, isolated and alone. Would meeting up years later make Serpil feel more at ease? She wasn't sure. Did she really want that? She was afraid of complicating what had already happened. Or perhaps only she thought that way.

She crossed the street and stood in front of the shop across from the restaurant. From there, since she could see the restaurant more clearly, she could think calmly. But as she observed the white awnings of the restaurant, she was filled with a sense of despair. Despite all their travels together and having lived together, the fact that she couldn't approach her friend pushed her deeper into misery. She turned onto the tree-lined road and pensively headed down to the town square.

\* \* \*

A cold sun emerged, and the lake became visible through the fog. She sat wearily on a stone bench. As she looked at the lake, various images of Serpil appeared in her mind:

In her eyes, a sea in the distance, an undulating, green sea; a foggy morning, she sat outside on the ferry. She watched the shore draw near.

Imaginings gave way to imaginings. In her mind, she began playing the game in which she and Serpil chance upon each other in a train compartment and start chatting.

In another reverie, Serpil places her arm in Behiye's arm, and they talk and laugh as they walk around an exhibition of paintings. Was it because Serpil was on the run that they went to those exhibitions, daytime cinema screenings and expositions? What are the things that people need to forget?

One day, paying no heed to the clouds overhead, they had gone from Istanbul to nearby Kınalı Island. That was such a lovely day. She compared the humble isolation of that space in front of her to the island's distance from the city. She could even smell the chill bitterness of the sea. Suddenly she remembered the letter that she always kept with her. She found it in her purse and took it out. Among the pages was a postcard: Kınalı island, its summit crowned by antennas. In the spring, they had gone to İzmir for Kemal's book signing. She had written the postcard there. She had wanted to surprise her friend, who had grown up in İzmir but now was living in places and with people she didn't know. She read it again; in the letter, she had given herself over to a flood of fancy and written of İzmir. The chirping of birds in the branches of tall eucalyptus trees slowly faded away. She sat on the bench, unable to move.

Then she envisioned Serpil sitting alone in the most secluded corner of a large restaurant. She was wearing a white jacket with glossy buttons. Her hair was in a ponytail. Her expression was the same as in the poster. She wasn't sad, but was lonely. To stave off her loneliness, she kept making the restaurant larger and larger. It was such that, in the end, the space in front of her became the restaurant, with its tables, chairs and paintings. The customers comfortably sat around in the cool light of the large dining hall and greeted each other over the flowers on the tables. Was Serpil smiling ever so slightly, like in the poster? She couldn't see her face clearly; Serpil was inside a tear drop.

After the sun disappeared behind a gray cloud, she got up from the bench. She folded up the papers in her hand and put them in her pocket. While passing through the square, she dug in her purse for a tissue. She waited for her tears to stop before getting in a taxi. Perhaps when there is grief like this, being at home or being abroad is one and the same.

# Evening from an Exeter Window

Semra Aktunç

*Translated by Mark David Wyers*

I keep thinking that perhaps Betty and that city, and its colors, sounds and silences, are fading from my memory. Perhaps. But whenever I look out a window, especially at night, details of that place gather in my mind's eye. As I remember the evenings in the south of that distant country, I envisage that windowsill upon which I used to lean as day faded into night. Truly, could it ever be forgotten?

In Exeter, dusk lingers for hours. When the rains abate, the evenings in July are bright and blue. As light gives way to darkness, the birds are stirred to passion, and the sky belongs to the evening. It gathers into itself other slices of time, balmy afternoons and crisp mornings.

Evening light is always a trickster, playing with colors and transforming the sky into a field for dreams. Even at this time, the red brick building across the way is so well lit that you can see the patterns of the lace curtains dancing in the cupboard mirror. When there is a light breeze, new figures join the dance.

Exeter, a city inhabited by over 100,000 people, was founded along the shores of the River Exe. We are guests in this city, staying in the same house and attending the same school. There are eight of us: Japanese, Italian, Swiss, Austrian, Spanish… We are a diminutive version of the United Nations.

The only person who takes language learning seriously is our host, Betty. She gives us pop quizzes, slips sly questions into her jokes, and corrects our mistakes with a smile. Peter, the Swiss student, sees her as the house teacher, and dotes on her every word, fearful of missing anything. He hopes to improve his English so that he can become more than just a humdrum banker. Even when tying his shoes he practices speaking. "I must learn," he says. He pronounces all of his "th"s like "z"s. "I think" becomes "I zink". Betty is patient; she will find a solution.

Maria the Italian is living it up and stays out all day and night. The Japanese student is polite, refined, silent. She moves around the house like a shadow, and even takes notes when we eat together. She has no interest whatsoever in watching television. If there is a problem with the lock on someone's valise, our Japanese housemate solves it in a snap, as if she speaks the language of locks and listens to their conversations with keys.

After dinner, we have "tea and talk time" with Betty. Betty and I especially enjoy these chats, and Peter, who doesn't speak much, even joins in sometimes, listening attentively. He is a clever chap; by listening to these conversations between Betty and this Turkish woman, he will learn much about the world. Peter has such a lovely smile, let him stay and listen, and in any case we don't talk about anything very private.

On some evenings Betty's glum daughter Dionne joins us. Betty beams, hoping that Dionne will join the chat and cheer up. This young woman had married twice and was abandoned both times, and she and her two sons live with Betty. Just like their mother, the boys are morose, rebellious and irritable.

The entire burden of running the household rests on Betty's shoulders, but she never loses her zest for life. She has contrived her own way to anaesthetize the unhappy times. For her, there is no such thing as an unsolvable problem. She sees only the bright side of things. And it is not just Betty; that whole generation of English men and women who lived through World War II are warm, friendly people. Of course not every era should have to undergo the tribulations of war, but that is how it is here. The youth are despondent, melancholic and rebellious, while the older generation has a youthful disposition that is upbeat and positive. There is such a vast difference between the two generations, and even though they are no further apart in age than a mother and daughter, it makes me wonder what happened in those twenty or thirty years.

Betty never speaks of the war when we all eat together, but when the others drift off to their rooms, she begins talking; she skips over the general facts because she knows that I am interested in her personal experiences and memories.

One afternoon during the war, she was outside when the air raid sirens began to wail. She ran, and just ahead she saw a young woman in a phone booth talking on the phone, smiling. Then suddenly the phone booth was incinerated by a bomb. For a moment Betty thought that she herself had died, and she stumbled along in shock until someone caught her by the arm and rushed her to a shelter.

"Everything was shrouded in something like smoke, fog or clouds, and I wandered among the rubble and the corpses of children, and there were noises, and there was silence," she says. As we talk, our friendship grows stronger and deeper. We can discuss with ease issues that we have never mentioned to anyone else. One night she said to me, "You are such a happy person." She lamented that she had not been able to teach her daughter how to laugh, that even as a child Dionne had been unhappy, and that she could see in her daughter's frightened eyes a heavy darkness.

I didn't say anything, couldn't find anything to say.

Betty's own marriage is blessed. She is still in love with her husband. During the war, he was taken prisoner in Burma and held captive for two years, and in those days he wrote letters to Betty every single day without fail. In this way, he was always in her life. She showed me the letters, and photographs as well, pictures of her and her husband dancing, dining and going on vacation. Betty was beautiful, and her husband handsome. Among the letters she found a gray ration card that had been issued to her during the war. Written on the card were the types and amounts of food she was allotted. I told Betty that the same information was written on my mother's and father's registration papers, and that although we hadn't entered the war, we had still gone through difficult times. Sympathy glistened in her eyes.

After this peace-loving generation has passed on, who will inherit this window, this enchantment of evening, this tranquility shimmering in red brick?

I remember that sometimes we would walk as far as the river; everywhere was so colorful, there were gardens, ponds, water lilies and fuchsias large as trees. Betty was grateful that she lived in a developed country, and at times would say, "We are lucky." But then she would talk about the high cost of living and go on about how even dying is an expensive affair. One day I saw her counting coins, and she explained that sometimes this was how she had to pay the bills. From that day on, I started putting my spare change into her tea tin, and she understood what I was doing and laughed but never said anything; embarrassment had no place in our friendship.

While the riverside was pleasant, getting back home involved a steep climb, so we would wait for one of those cars they call a "busy bee" to whisk us home in just ten minutes.

When she found out that I was keeping a journal, Betty became determined that each day I should take in all that I could of life in England. She made sure that we took advantage of every moment; sometimes she would drop her work, change her clothes, and off we would go to explore. But, she never forgot to put on her pearl necklace before setting out.

It was on such a day that we went to a private service being held in the main chamber of the cathedral. For some reason, Betty was quite excited about this. The bishop, visiting from Aberdeen, was delivering a long sermon laced with humor, and the congregation of about 150 people listened, laughing whenever he made a joke. At one point the bishop approached me and placed a small copy of *The English Hymnal* in my hands, looking into my eyes with love and compassion. Betty was ecstatic, but I didn't understand why; was this bishop someone important? After the sermon, the bishop approached me again, and I could tell that he knew I was a foreigner. He shook my hand, clasping it for a long time, and said "Peace be with you." I thanked him, and we smiled at each other. Betty's face was beaming, aglow with pride like a mother feels for her child. For me as well, the way that the venerated bishop had behaved towards me carried a special meaning.

Going to Sunday church is a thousand times better than dawdling in front of the television. Particularly in that quiet city, sharing exciting moments is an opportunity that should never be missed.

I can still feel the spirit of nobility of the city, a nobility that tries to conceal so much within but is dying, being forgotten. Aside from Betty, how many English people would understand me on this point?

At times, Betty spoke of the pity she felt for the generations to come. I asked if there was no hope, and she replied that there is, but it will only be possible on another planet where people live a in a way that we cannot comprehend. She believed this with all of her being, saying that she was too old at that point to change her mind. When you discussed "the future" with this woman who was so positive and fearless and who accepted and loved life just as it was, fear and anxiety overtook her.

Evening. Dark is settling over everything. I can still feel that tranquil breeze. What is the cause of Betty's concerns for the future? Her daughter, grandchildren?

That sense of peace that I carry within, what does it mean for the other people living in this city? What is it in itself? Betty, isn't this what we need to talk about?

Again it is evening and I am at my window.

It is raining.

Years have passed.

I no longer receive letters from Betty.

I have kept all of the letters she sent, along with the rations card she gave me.

My last night in Exeter we talked, and even wept, but there was one thing she said which I will never forget. It still sends a chill down my spine: "If you stop receiving letters from me, know that I am no longer in this world."

# My Dear Compatriot

Nurhayat Bezgin

*Translated by Mark David Wyers*

I was exhausted but got to bed quite late, so I didn't sleep well. To make matters worse, I was the first presenter in the morning. I got up early and turned on my computer. After glancing through the news, my plan was to get some work done.

As I sifted through the online newspapers, I was thinking, "Well, let's just have a look at what's happening back home and in the rest of the world. What will the second week of March bring us?" My heart froze at one story.

An earthquake, 6.0 on the Richter scale, the epicenter located in the village of Karakoçan in Elazığ, in the east of Turkey. More than fifty estimated casualties.

That night, when my eyes fell upon the sundry packages I had put on the sofa, I felt even worse. It was as if, understanding what had happened, they sat there in mourning.

\* \* \*

Ms. Brigitte is one of three nurses at the glimmering white health center. She is a multilingual, tender-hearted nurse. She has become like a friend who takes close care of all of the health problems of the trainees, who are constantly coming and going. Perhaps to improve work efficiency, she was deployed far from large cities in the heart of nature, a star of the organization.

"Ms. Çiçek," she said, smiling, "The doctor will call you in shortly. But if you will allow me, there is something I would like to say."

I was surprised and alarmed at the same time. In a foreign country, what could a nurse I was seeing for the first time have to say to me? Or did the situation seem grave? Well, I hadn't paid much attention to the fatigue brought on by a simple two-day cold. When she saw my surprise, she said, "Don't worry," as she passed me a glass of steaming fruit tea. "Ms. Berfin Vollenweider and her family, who are registered at our center, live here. She is a very dear friend of mine. She always talks about how she misses her home country. When I found out that you are from Turkey, I wanted to ask you if you would like to meet her. You see... This is the first time I have met a Turkish trainee."

I wanted to hug and kiss her. On the other side of the world, she was asking politely if she could introduce me to a compatriot.

"Of course," I said. "Thank you, Ms. Brigitte. If you could give me her phone number, I will get in touch with her right away."

"That wouldn't do at all!" she said, a glimmer in her green eyes. "Berfin will be ecstatic. She'll call you whenever you wish."

\* \* \*

A month had passed since arriving at Studienzentrum. We were staying at a small housing unit in Seftigen, a region in the canton of Bern in Switzerland. Gerzensee, just like the glimmering lake for which it was named, was stunning.

I was one of the trainees from an international bank. My nine fellow trainees were, like me, upper-level bankers from various countries. What was it that brought us together? This small region that brightened our spirits and filled us with enthusiasm like children, or the stressful working conditions driven by competition? We weren't able to answer that question. But every day we impatiently waited for five o'clock, to quickly change our clothes and explore the area. Sometimes we walked, but usually we cycled to take in the area's sights. Sometimes we even ventured out before breakfast.

We were staying in a vast plain near fields that had begun turning green. The Alps never ceased to astound us, with their slopes nourished by the runoff from the mountain peaks. Ruddy health radiated from the faces of the women and men cultivating this fertile land, the population of which is said to not even exceed one thousand. We met some of them and chatted. They were friendly people. I don't know if it was because we were foreign, but they were very cordial with us. The villages and homes were tidy, just like the people. The schools, churches and especially the health center were all spotless, well-lit buildings.

The houses with broad verandas, known as country homes, usually had small barns in the back. In the large gardens, they did organic farming, probably just for the family. Clearly the plump housewives with braided hair were in charge of these gardens.

On the streets of Gerzensee, we almost never came across children or young people. Of course I wasn't surprised when I found out that the youth, of which there were few anyway, were either in school, doing sports, or studying art.

\* \* \*

The subjects of our work and research are economic models, financial techniques and developing countries. My country, Turkey, is among those countries which used to be referred to as "developing" but are now known as "emerging markets". Turkey has been developing for years, and praised as if it were emerging, but unfortunately it has been defined in various terms of underdevelopment. The topic of the day during breaks is, of course, Haiti. The fact that thousands of earthquake victims have been buried beneath the rubble is a source of grief for everyone.

Once, our professor from Harvard noted, "The problem is not just about incorrect structures. Look, most of the buildings here are prefabricated. They have been designed and manufactured in harmony with the local conditions. Particularly in regions prone to earthquakes, this should most definitely be borne in mind."

Straight away they began asking me questions. After the disaster in Istanbul, were precautions undertaken? Has migration to the city been reduced? The fault line in northern Anatolia has been active. How is the housing in mountainous regions being constructed?

I wish I could give a positive answer to their questions. If only I could say, without pangs of grief and a twinge in my heart:

"Everything is fine now. Because the necessary precautions were taken and are being taken…"

* * *

When Berfin said, "Dear, I am just dying to see you," her voice was full of warmth. It was as though her words were trembling with forty years of longing. "I'll come at ten?"

I smiled. Ah, my dear Berfin, the accented voice of my Anatolia. She doesn't ask "Shall I come at ten?" She just says "I'll come at ten?" and her voice rises at the end. I want to say "Of course that's fine," but at the same time I am thinking "But of course you must!" It is clear that she is a working woman and that her husband will be at home. Her one day to rest at home together with her children… She must have sensed my hesitation, because she insisted:

"Nurhan, don't worry that tomorrow is Sunday. Hans and the children really would like to meet you."

"Okay then," I said, "We'll have our morning coffee here, together."

\* \* \*

After making the arrangements with Berfin, I looked at my watch; it was still early. At noon, we were going to go to Bern, thirty minutes away. Thinking of taking a rest, I went out onto the balcony, drawing my shawl over my shoulders. At that moment it was like I had become one with nature as it glimmered through the spring sunshine.

*From far away, the sound of bells chiming. They are taking the fattened herds to graze. On the neat roads, the sheep are at the head, trundling along without raising their heads. Then behind them come the black-eyed cattle, to be grazed on special pastures to plump their udders with milk. Chewing their cud, they plod in an orderly way ahead of the cheery herdsmen. They don't even leave a mess behind, much less raise dust, because of the sweeper car that follows behind.*

*"Just like our herds!" I imagine. In my dream, I see the well-fed animals alongside our wealthy (!) herders.*

*The villagers, most of whom are landowners, have begun work. Wiry men wearing broad hats to protect them from the sun ride their horses at an amble. Attractive women in denim sit astride tractors. The pleasant-faced people working the vast fields neatly divided into plots wave at me from afar. After finishing work, they will get into their new cars parked in front of their flower-bedecked houses and go down to the town. Or, as a weekly tradition, they will enjoy a fondue at one of the nearby restaurants.*

*"This is their natural right," my dream voice says. And it adds, "Just like in Turkey (!), they are granted a special subsidy." They remain in their vil-*

*lages, and because they work in agriculture and livestock, they are held in high regard. Neither wind nor flood can sweep away what they produce. The rewards of all this labor remain in the hands of the workers and are not just left in the fields. Reaping season arrives, and people come to collect it, paying up front in fruits and vegetables, or barley and wheat…*

* * *

As the attendant at the door looked on in surprise, Berfin and I hugged and kissed like old friends. Were we weeping or laughing? It wasn't clear. But a strange dampness glistened on our faces and in our eyes.

"Come on," Berfin says, "let's get going." Laughing, she says, "My car is like me, no?" as we get into the large station wagon.

This olive-skinned woman is right. Indeed, she is solidly built. Everything about Ms. Vollenweider reflects the vigor of youth: the jet-black hair in a thick braid hanging down her back, the glinting eyes beneath her thick eyebrows, her straight, powerful figure.

I notice right away that she has an ebullient personality. There is so much she wants to explain and show to me. The speedometer in the car is just like her talk. Once in a while she reaches out and holds my hand or strokes my back. She asks if it angers me that she calls me *abla*, older sister. Of course not, why would it?

"Is it noticeable, abla?" she asks, melancholy creeping into her voice. "All of the difficult things I have been through since I was a child?"

She explains that her father had come as a laborer to the capital of Switzerland from the village of Karakoçan in Elazığ. "When he forgot about his wife in the village and married that damn Helga, he settled down and stayed here for good," she says. Then, one by one, he brought his children, and in Berfin's words, "made men of all of them." She had begun to fall in love with Hans when he was still a middle-school student at the Oberstufenschule. "But it wasn't just me, he was in love with me too," she beams. After they got married, they moved onto Hans' father's property. Even though they have their own fields, she explained with some embarrassment, they actually work as laborers. But she didn't forget to proudly add, "Around here, abla, most people are like us anyway."

I ask if she has any relatives aside from her mother in her village, which she had only visited twice in all of these years. Her eyes pensive, she answers, "Yes. There is my older sister Zeliş, she actually resembles you a little." With a sigh, the cause of which I would understand only later, she says, "My dearly departed mother passed on her coy Circassian side to my sister, and I was left with my father's hard-working Kurdishness." We both laugh.

"But she couldn't bear to leave mother, and she stayed in the village," she says, a secret note of pride in her voice for the sister she missed. She also has a number of nephews trying to eke out a living on the rooftops of the village houses made from adobe.

She adds with a hint of shame that she sends money to her family there just once in a while, but says, "At least, thankfully, the children are going to school." Actually, she is quite upset with her family there. When I ask why, she explains:

"The man who would be my brother-in-law left everything and joined the Kurdish guerillas in the mountains, leaving the children in poverty. In the villages, there were so many things, so many things to do... But not a single man to work. The ones that are left just chase after the women," she says, with a bitter laugh. "What are they going to do with so many children, with no home, no hearth?" she complains.

"You know better than me," she says. "Our people are so lazy, such sloths! Can you just expect the government to do everything? They should come here and see what it means to work." Her father understood the value of land when he came, but what good came of it? His mind, it seems, was all about the city.

Chatting and sharing our grief, we drive around for quite a while. Then she takes me to a cozy rest stop. I think that as we enjoy our *gebäck* pastries and coffee, she is surprised at my admiration as I gaze upon the view of the beautiful snow-capped mountains perfectly reflected in the still waters of the lake.

"Do you really think so?" she asks, a twinge of reproach in her voice. "I am sure you have never seen our village before." At that moment I think to myself, "What does a spoiled city woman know about the beauty of villages?" She doesn't ask who I am, where I am from. But when I realize what Berfin's real concern is, I feel ashamed.

She is wondering, when will I return to Turkey, and would I happen to pass through Elazığ?

"My dear…" I say, looking into her eyes. "If there is anything you would like me to do or anything you would like to send, don't hesitate to tell me." She is overjoyed, my dear compatriot. "Okay then," she says, jumping up with joy. And I follow.

"First, let's buy some presents for my sister," she says, "after that we can go to my house."

# Disco Brazil

Tezer Özlü

*Translated by Alvin Parmar*

The Mediterranean is a different kind of blue. Especially on a sunny day in May. The train goes past tiny towns. I'm looking at the sea. It's misty. Blue. There's something so saturated, so deep, so immense about it. It's practically pulling me in. And its calmness is relaxing. People keep getting on and off the train. Fat or thin Italians with tanned and dry, careworn faces that show how hard they have to work for a living but that they have lost none of their vitality and humanity. I talk to some of them from time to time. I look at the sea. I go out into the corridor and look at the stations we stop at, at what's around, at the buildings, their balconies, the flowers in pots adorning the balconies, or at the garbage that's been thrown out onto the balconies, the clothes hung up to dry, at the window that's been left ajar, at the person looking out the window, at the small cars going down the road, at the people standing at a corner, at the people walking down the pavements, at the people riding bikes, at the full cafes and the empty cafes, at the small child holding a grown-up's hand, at the priests that appear from time to time, or at the nuns walking in groups. Then I see a class of schoolchildren, and it occurs to me that I have nothing in common with the people of this small town and that maybe I'll remember nothing about it. The train moves

on. After twenty miles of towns, it's suddenly France. I don't remember
how much longer it took me to get to Nice, but it wasn't particularly
late when I got there, somewhere around noon. I'm sitting with Zelda
on her balcony. There's a nice warmth. You know, the warmth of the
first warm day of the year. Cigarettes even taste different. You can
smoke them without any bitter taste at the end. Past the buildings rising up around the house, lush green mountains begin. Except for the
seafront, every part of the city is enclosed by these mountains and their
lush green. From the balcony, the seafront has vanished in a thick mist.
Even if there was no mist, I still don't think you'd be able to see the
sea from here. I'm tired, but the thought of going to the esplanade, the
desire to see that wide palm-lined boulevard that I'd heard about for
years, won't leave me. Apart from the greenness and the white or pale-
colored houses, I don't know what kind of a city I'm in yet. A few hours
later, I'm walking along the wide boulevard towards the sea.

Shop, shop, shop, on the corner or shoved in between two buildings
a cafe, another shop, a bigger shop, on the other side of the road, big
famous shops and another cafe, another shop, traffic lights, junctions,
intense human and vehicular traffic, I'm in a crowd that's in a hurry,
filling all available space (and I still haven't reached the sea). I come to
a big park. I think I'm coming to the end of this boulevard that runs
along both sides of the park straight down to the sea. I wonder if I
should walk through the park or go around it. When I notice there
are very old people sitting very sedately in it, I decide to stay on the
boulevard. I come to another boulevard, even wider than a square.
Immediately beneath a very wide pedestrian zone there are stony
beaches where thousands of sun loungers await people to lie on them.
Here in the mist with the open Mediterranean behind. So this is the
Riviera, the place that years of American, French, Italian, or joint

French-Italian films has crystallized in my mind. Evening approaches. I'm very tired. If I just took a dip in the sea, I know my head, weary from all these scenes, could relax. But no one swims at this time of day. I'll have to wait until tomorrow morning. Opposite the multitudinous sun loungers are gardens with rows of very large buildings in them. On the street level, they have luxury cafes and shops. The city is made up of boulevards that run parallel with the Mediterranean and others that transect them. They are lined with gardens with very large buildings, *résidences*, in them. In one area, all the buildings are named after composers: Beethoven House, Chopin House, Mozart, Mendelssohn and so on. In another area, they're all named after writers: Balzac House, Zola… None of the buildings has been named after a modern writer yet; maybe there's still time, I think.

When you turn your back to the sea and have the city in front of you, you'll see that the whole left side is the product of a similar affluence. It stretches up to the mountains behind; then because of the sky, I don't know where it goes after that.

The ostentatious, well-fed rich of Western Europe and America fill the boulevards, cafes and shops here. Another thing you notice in this part of town is women old enough to be called fossils because they have exceeded the natural human lifespan, wandering around, all dolled up, with a pedigree dog or doddering old man in tow. Germans drive the biggest and most expensive models of Mercedes here. In any case, American space explorers have proved that the moon isn't as romantic and beautiful a place as it seemed. It's actually a desolate, mountainous shithole full of lakes of solitude. So what are Germans or rich Americans going to do on the moon? Where can rich Germans and Americans, and tourists from the leading or not so leading Common Market countries go? Nice, of course. Cannes. Where do they create fashion for? Who will fashion houses sell their wares to? Hermes? Dior? Chanel? Cacharel? And smelly cheese? To the elite in Nice, of course.

Anyway, you're in Nice and you're in the Disco Brazil. It's on the right-hand side of town, a patchwork of poor neighborhoods. The streets are old and narrow, the houses are multicolored and as old as the streets. There are lively little cafes. Small shops put their goods out on the streets. You can find trousers being sold next to fish. One of Saint Mary's who knows how many graves (the tourist may be mistaken here, she wandered around without a guide or city map) stands silently between two collapsed buildings, in anonymity where the steep, poor streets come to an end. The buildings here don't have names. A different family lives in each room. If you peek through the half-open doors, the dank, dilapidated corridors and stairs smell of damp. A few geraniums have been put in tin canisters in front of the windows, laundry has been hung from one side of the street to the other. All the blacks are housed around here. Young girls with dyed hair, platform heels and bell-bottom jeans sit in front of the doors. Maybe they tell each other love stories and (ah!) the necessity or the possibility or the impossibility of escaping from this life, from living like sardines in the old neighborhoods of Nice.

They're well dressed and pretty. In Western Europe's consumer society, it's almost impossible not to be well dressed. Anyone seeing these girls strolling along the Riviera wouldn't be able to tell which social class they were from. And yes, maybe tourists are the richest class in the Riviera. But what is a tourist? Does a tourist develop in or develop the country that they visit? Or is it their muscles they develop as they lift their heavy suitcase from the station platform to board a second-class carriage on a train to another country? Or maybe they

develop a thirst and raise a glass in Disco Brazil. To the good health of
the young people of Martinique! Young people from French-exploited
Martinique (what an apt description that is: EXPLOITATION) dance
in Disco Brazil in Nice. They have dancing in their veins. They dance
their liveliest, most beautiful dances when they don't have a girl at their
side (as if they're used to not having girls) in Disco Brazil in Nice.

The disco is where the wide Riviera coast and the palm trees reach
their highest point, a single story building with the poor neighborhoods extending behind it. Large windows descend to the level of the
pavement. Apart from a small bar where you have to stand, the tables
and low chairs have been laid out neatly. Music doesn't play by itself
from a sound system here. The clientele has to put money in the jukebox
and pay to dance, a form of "he who pays the piper calls the tune". But
they're generous and they're always feeding change into the jukebox so
there won't be a break in the music. The Martiniquais dance with youth,
naturalness and a sense of determined resistance. No one else, not even
a dance champion, could keep up with the music so naturally. Long
live the Riviera! Long live Nice! Long live Disco Brazil! Long live the
exploited peoples! May they live long so they can be exploited, may
they be exploited so they can pay money and dance? May they dance!

And Ilyas:

Ilyas is a young French man. Tall and thin. With protruding ears,
big, slightly bulging dark eyes, and a bony jaw. He immediately stands
out among the black people. He's come to Disco Brazil this night after
a day when everyone's been in the sea and under the hot sun. He's
wearing a canvas coat, with a wool scarf around his neck and canvas
shoes on his feet.

There's no sign of a shirt or sweater from below the sleeves of the
overcoat; he might be naked underneath it. His strange dancing imme-

diately catches your eye. He focuses on his hand and arm movements, then he leaps like a ballet dancer, bends to the ground, then folds his arms and comes up like a statue. Compared to the others, he can't dance to save his life, but every so often he pulls off a dance move with his canvas-shod feet that makes you think the Martiniquais have got nothing on him. Then he loses his way again, messes things up and attracts attention for his ineptitude. I notice at one point that his chair is very close to mine. We talk a bit. He's eighteen. He tells me he walks six kilometers there and back to come here. He starts work at seven in the morning and does the filing in an office until a quarter to four. He earns one thousand new francs. He says he lived in Paris for a time but didn't like it there at all. He was very lonely. He's very happy on the Riviera. He has a brother around here too; he can see him from time to time if he wants. (I don't think his brother particularly likes dancing.) The Martiniquais put some more money in the jukebox. The frenetic songs wipe out all the thoughts in your head. One singer's shouting at the top of his lungs. In the streetlights on the boulevard, there are so many cars. Everyone's running to the dance floor. There are two French girls dancing with each other now too.

"I have to dance to this song," says Ilyas. He pulls a fantastic move with one foot on the other knee.

On my way home after midnight, I notice Ilyas on the opposite side of the road walking, talking to two of the locals.

"Ah, Ilyas!" I say. I immediately think of the six kilometers he has to walk and I ask him how he'll get up and go to work in the morning.

The boulevard is lit. The sea is behind me. I'm walking in the mountain area. The streets are empty. Now and then a car goes past. And in one or two places a small group of tourists pops up. There are people playing table tennis in the few cafes that are still open. Come morning, every corner of the city will be full. Tourists, locals and fossils will come out of the named houses or the staircases that smell of damp and start the day in the beautiful early-summer heat. And I'm going to go swimming with Zelda. Zelda has lived in Nice for three years. Her only friend is her fat cat.

# The Face in the Photo

Menekşe Toprak

*Translated by Alvin Parmar*

So physical objects did change form depending on how you felt; they gained other meanings: streets became cheerful, buildings became historical not old, sooty colors blended into white, the smell of the linden trees no longer seemed suffocating, on the contrary, it turned into a soothing summer smell. If she had not been holding some photos, she could have clapped her hands with glee like a child now. It was as if the sky, cleansed of its ashen color after a night of rain, was bright blue; physical objects had lost some of their hardness in this mild weather; the smells wafting from the linden trees in every corner of the city had been refreshed.

She stood in a corner of the square; she looked at the big round clock on the bus shelter opposite the subway entrance. Her eye went to the relief on the façade of the subway building, said to be one of the oldest stations in the city, and from there to the building's transparent glass roof that looked like the dome of a mosque. It was strange, but everything struck her as beautiful this morning. More beautiful than ever before. She had even forgotten the stress at the photographer's just now. She had tensed up when the photographer said, "Please smile a little! Maybe some makeup would liven up your face". Actually, she was surprised that she had understood him at all; if you were going to smile, did your heart not have to smile too? A photographer whose hair had turned gray ought to have known that. Still, she tried to smile by remembering that she was making a new start in life with these passport photos she was having taken. Had she succeeded, or had the photographer, in spite of all his efforts, finally settled for the imitation smile she had managed to muster by trying to wriggle her mouth and face? In the end he said, "That's great now!" and pressed the button a few times.

She tried to suppress the nervousness that rose from inside her as she fingered the envelope with the photos in it. It was a good start; the mild weather and the clear sky were signs that she would make a good start.

She was walking towards the bus stop where she was to meet Rukiye, but she looked at the clock again and changed her mind. She turned around. It was not even nine thirty yet; it would be at least another half hour until Rukiye came.

There were so many cafes and restaurants on the street that stretched out in front of her. Not to mention all the people sitting at the tables outside at this time of the morning on a weekday, without a care in the world, like they did not have to worry about anything like work. Mehmet too—she did not know where he had spent the night—had probably sat in one of these cafes before going to work. Mehmet, who did not come home at night, and who buried himself in his own silent world with a sullen, sorrowful expression when he did come, would only manage a few disjointed words. He would always have been hanging out with his friends, and would have had his breakfast in a cafe if he had been out until morning. From now on, she was not going to get upset at him for doing that. From now on, she was not going to blame herself for how he mournfully curled up at the far side of the bed, and she was not going to think about which house or dark alley, which bar, for there were none he had not been to in the city, which nightclub, he kept running away from her to, living a completely separate life.

The cafe with a blue awning at the corner of the street opposite the bus stop caught her eye. She liked the orange chairs. A cup of coffee, a cigarette... And should she get a copy of *Hürriyet* from the newsstand at the subway entrance? Today is a good day. Maybe her stars today would say that too. But she changed her mind; she had spent a large part of the thirty Euros she earned from her cleaning job this morning on cigarettes and on the passport photos she had in her hand now.

She was just stepping out to cross the road when there was a skidding noise accompanied by rattling and screeching, followed by the hurried sound of a bell ringing and the raucous voice of a woman yelling "Vorsicht!" She stepped back. She had not seen the woman on the bike, and it was only now that she noticed she was walking in the cycle lane. The woman's long, curly red hair was billowing backwards in the same rhythm as the multi-colored skirt that she was wearing. Her long, shapely bare legs were uncovered up to the thigh. When the woman turned around and irritatedly said a few incomprehensible things as she rode off, she felt like swearing at the cyclist, like reeling off all the swearwords she knew in this language. But she immediately let it go; today was a good day; today she was going to start a new life.

Sipping on the coffee the server had put down in front of her, she opened her bag and took out a transparent folder. It contained her navy blue passport complete with its barely dry, two-year unlimited residence stamp and the flimsy paper of her two-page work permit, as well as her high school diploma with its stylized drawing of Atatürk. Actually, the diploma would have to be translated into German too, but the woman on the phone had said there was no hurry. And the passport photos she had just had done. Ah, and if only she was not so nervous, if only she did not have these cramps in her stomach. But most of all, she wanted to be free of this feeling of guilt that stood in the way of her doing anything decisive, this feeling that was already dragging her into its vortex; was it a pang of conscience? Or fear? Or a yearning? Were people not wracked with this much yearning when they were separated from their dogs or even when they were moving house? This must be something like that. Nothing more. The door she was standing in front of, did it really lead to a new life? Would she be able to step through it?

A little later, she would meet up with Rukiye and the woman who ran the Turkish care home that had changed Rukiye's life, enabled her to escape from that terrible husband of hers and helped her get her residence and work permits. And what's more, Rukiye had been saying, you've already got an unlimited residence and work permit, like a window of opportunity; you'll definitely get the job.

If she did take the job, from now on she would be cleaning old and sick Turkish people's houses, cooking them food, bathing them, cutting their nails and giving them their medication. But that was not all; she would be cleaning up the ones who were bedridden. Rukiye had said, "You need to get well prepared for this job! You'll be putting diapers on the asses of wrinkly grannies and grandpas in their eighties who shit themselves; you'll have to stomach the stench; that's the most difficult thing. But you'll get used to it. Instead of dealing with the shit your husband gives you every day, isn't it more honorable for you to earn your money cleaning other people's? Besides, it's the only window of opportunity, the only job prospect in this country for people like us."

People like us? They had both come to this country as brides. Ru-kiye four years ago, and she six. Long enough for her to forget her old life, in fact. But her own story had absolutely nothing in common with what Rukiye had gone through! Nothing at all. She had only been beaten once by Mehmet, right at the beginning of their marriage. She was still a newlywed; she had just come over from Turkey. She had asked Mehmet why he did not go to the doctor. That was all! But soft, mostly silent Mehmet had moved in on her, his face flushed, the veins on his neck standing out and throbbing, and he had hit her with all his might. "I never wanted you!" he yelled. "They lumbered me with you! They forced you to become a burden around my neck!" he raged. "I'm a healthy man. You should see how many girls there've been in my life, how many hot German girls. If it's not happening with you, it's because I don't love you." If she had not said, "Then why didn't you just keep on fucking them then, what did you want with me?" she would not have been on the receiving end of that terrible beating that day. No, no, her situation still was nothing like Rukiye's. What a terrible story Rukiye had. Her husband had even shoved her head down the toilet a few times. He would apparently lock her in the house so she could not get out. Some days the poor thing was alone like that at home with no food or water. But how relaxed she is when she talks about all of that. Even the sadistic things he used to do to her in bed... No, she said to herself, no, my situation has absolutely nothing in common with Rukiye's. You have just got to be careful not to strike any of Mehmet's raw nerves, not to press him about where he went, what he was doing, what he spent where, and once in a blue moon do what he wants you to do in bed. And that is all.

She took out her navy blue passport from the folder and opened the first page. How young she was in the photo with her long hair! When she was eighteen, her hair was full of curls, her lips and cheeks had a rosy glow. She looked a little shy. She had been so nervous when she was having it taken. Musa Amca, the local photographer, had said that her bridal photo should be pretty even if it was a passport photo. Actually, that time too, when she was having her photo taken on her own for the first time, she had thought about being on the threshold of a new life and got nervous and jittery trying to imagine what that distant, unknown world might be like. After all, she was going as a bride to a foreign country very, very far away from the slums they lived in.

The couple having breakfast at the table right next to her caught her eye. The man, who was sitting with his back to her, had short hair that was completely white. As the woman sitting opposite him leaned forwards, her breasts, visible from the low-cut neckline of her strappy floral dress, came together to form a cleavage; as she leant back, her breasts suddenly sagged down and the cleavage disappeared. The wrinkles on her long neck, indistinct marks on her tanned, freckled skin, the loose skin that was starting to form around her throat… How old could she be? Fifty, fifty-five? It was as if the man and the woman were lovesick teenagers. He would bring a slice of bread he had spread jam on up to her lips, touch it against them then pull it back; she would look for the bread with her mouth, look at him provocatively, and then bite into the bread.

Will I ever be able to experience anything like that? Will I be able to be play around like that with a man?

"Why not?" Rukiye had said recently. "You're so pessimistic, like an old woman. But you're still only twenty-five. We've still got our whole life in front of us."

Was it really true? How and from where did Rukiye get her strength, her optimism?

Yes, yes, Rukiye's right, she thought to herself. If I land this job, I'll sit Mehmet down and we'll talk like two adults, yes, yes, not as his wife, but as his friend. I'm not a child, she was going to say. And I'm certainly not an ignorant woman. In Turkey, I finished high school. And with good marks, too. If I hadn't married you and come here, maybe I'd have gone to university, and I'd have long since graduated by now too. But I'm not holding that against you. I understand that you don't love me, she was going to say. I understand it's not just me, but that you won't be able to love any woman. You were the one who was forced to touch a body you didn't want to touch, she would say. You were forced to get married; I was cheated, she was going to add. Actually, I was bursting with joy when you asked for my hand, she was going to confess. I was going to go to a country with a language and ways I didn't know. I wasn't even eighteen; you said I'd learn German, maybe have a career. Then we were going to have children. One girl, one boy. Yes, that's right. You who puts to shame film stars with your good looks, with your face that was a little more handsome each year when you came to visit, and you chose me from among all the friends' and relatives' daughters in the neighborhood who were crazy about you. I always loved you, she was going to say, your handsome face, the way you took care of yourself, your silent and dignified bearing. But it didn't work out. You've got to live how you want to from now on. I'm not a stupid woman; I know you'll never love me, she was going to say. God created you like that. But that'll be our secret, no one, no one at all will ever find out, not your family or mine, she was going to say.

She might even have been able to convince Mehmet to tell their families, but how were they supposed to do that? Her mother-in-law would say, see, she got her residence and work permit thanks to us and now she's left my son high and dry. She would nag, if you'd had a child, Mehmet dear, she'd have been tied down. They would berate her, if you'd been a real woman! What her mother had said when they went to visit a few years ago rang in her ears: "Dear, just look at the state you're in! That beautiful hair of yours…" And she stopped. Her mother, who never wanted to stir up any trouble, who was convinced that a woman just had to grin and bear whatever bad things fate might have in store for her, had looked at her in anguish for a moment, tears had come to her eyes, then she had looked away. That determined black veil had descended over her eyes because she had not wanted to join up the dots, she had not wanted to know the reasons behind her daughter's new, ever-deteriorating condition, she had chosen not to probe, not even to scratch the wound behind the silence that, while discreet, could still erupt at any moment nonetheless. As if she would be able to tell her mother if she asked her what was wrong!

Suddenly a shadow fell across her; it grew wider and darker. She looked up. The clouds had piled up in the sky; they were spreading out quickly. The sky on the other side of the subway station, though, was still blue. An old woman was getting out of the yellow double-decker bus at the bus stop where she was going to meet Rukiye. A man reached out his hand to help her get out. After the bus had moved off, the woman, who was at least eighty and hunchbacked, stayed where she was, leaned on her stick to straighten herself up, looked all around like she wanted to select a course, then narrowed her eyes and focused on the pavement opposite the cafe where she was sitting. In the direction where the old woman had pointed her curious, scandalized glance, two men were walking with their hands all over each other; every so often they would slow down and kiss each other on the lips.

And wasn't it around here where she had seen Sergio, an old friend of Mehmet? Hand in hand with a man at least six feet tall, thick-set and with a shaven head. When their eyes met, Sergio had quickly looked down at the ground and turned his face the other way. He was Mehmet's closest friend; he would call every day and would turn up at their house at all hours, pick up Mehmet and be off. When she saw him hand in hand with a man like that, she could not believe her eyes, but at the same time, it was as if suddenly everything started falling into place. It was as if fake dark worlds that she had not been able to define until that day, and that she had never given any thought to and did not want to think about had suddenly been spread out wide open in front of her. She thought she had worked out the meaning of Mehmet's agitated, strained touches, of the unease in his tightly curled-up body at the far side of the bed, of those rare times they had increasingly brusque, loveless sex that ended as soon as it began and that always seemed to be performed out of duty, of the look he always had on his face after he had come that made her feel he was overflowing with disgust and regret. It was completely instinctive. Could she have told him how she bumped into Sergio? She had not been able to tell him at the time and she would not be able to talk about it now. All she had been able to do at the time was say she had seen Sergio in the street, one time Mehmet was at the table picking at his food in silence and without appetite, but she had not been able tell him the rest.

She thought she saw Mehmet's face go bright red, his fingers holding the spoon pause and tremble… Who had been hurt the most that day? Mehmet, who in all probability had found out long, long ago that Sergio, who had not been around for weeks, was with another man? Or was it her, who understood for the first time that her husband was suffering the pain of love for another man?

It was getting darker and darker; the clouds in the sky had reached the subway building too now and you could actually see them spreading to the far reaches of the city. Rukiye was still nowhere to be seen, but it must have been getting close to ten o'clock. It was time she got up. She put the passport and the other documents into the folder. It was two photos they had asked for for the job application, wasn't it?

She took the photos out of the envelope. The photographer had given them a cursory glance before putting them in. She took one of them in her hand and looked at it closely. She froze. Was the person in the photo her? Were they hers, those thin dry lips opened in order to smile but frozen into an anomalous, foreign grin, those untidy eyebrows that had not seen tweezers for years, and those brown, sorrowful eyes looking out with a stony expression from under her eyebrows? No mirror had revealed the change she had gone through over the years, but now this real face of hers in the photo, with short hair like a man and protruding cheekbones was looking at her. And she thought of Mehmet saying in the first days of their marriage when they had just come here that he hated makeup and that her thick, long black hair did not suit her at all, and him sitting her down in a hairdresser's chair; she thought of his bulging body taking her from behind the same evening and she could not stop the tears flowing from her eyes and rolling quickly down her cheeks.

Now she could hear the raindrops on the awning above her; the pavement was quickly getting wet and changing color. She looked across the road with moist eyes. The sky was dark; the subway building, lashed by the rain, had taken on a dark smoky color, its transparent dome had disappeared beneath the dark sky. Rukiye, who was standing waiting under the canopy of the bus shelter, was playing with her long, light brown hair. There was a blond man walking along without taking his eyes off her; she looked at him with a shy expression just as he was going past, then she turned her head towards the clock again and looked around, annoyed. She, though, was examining from a distance Rukiye's feminine way of standing and the wedge heels of the shoes she was wearing with jeans; never mind throwing the documents on the table into her bag and going to meet her now, she did not even want to be here. She just wanted to go away, to run away to somewhere where nobody knew her.

# Short Stories: Apprentices of Life Abroad

Zeynep Avcı

*Translated by Mark David Wyers*

## 1.

I had a friend (even though I haven't seen him for a long time, I still think of him as a friend). Our country was going through rough times, and the blows of the coup battered him as well. He found a way out and fled to a quiet country in Europe. His sallow wife, however, hadn't dared take that step. He was alone. Trying to keep a low profile, he slipped into the bustle of a city. Although he held degrees from two universities, he was resigned to whatever work he could find and he managed to make some money. But after a year, loneliness had descended upon him. He became enamored of a curly-haired woman and took his chances on another adventure. The woman had it in her mind that she was going to have children with a good man. And she did. Twins, at that: a boy and a girl. But the twins were too much for her. She plucked him from his job and shuttled him off to a village. While he went about trying to find work, his wife comfortably settled into her mother's home with the twins. For a few months, the curly-haired woman, her widowed mother, and the twins and husband managed to get along. Finally having gotten their hands on a man, however, they piled him up with work. Singlehandedly, he overhauled the run-down country home. From the fuses to the plumbing, they had everything repaired without paying a cent. When the twins turned ten months old, he was still jobless. On one of those days when the autumn rains begin, the curly-haired woman sat the man down opposite her and explained that they just couldn't feed two babies and a grown man on her widowed mother's salary. Since he couldn't find work in the village, it would be better if he went back to the city. And he did, once more starting from scratch. He was alone, again. For a couple of years, he got to see the twins once every few months. But he hasn't seen them for twenty-eight years. He doesn't even know where they live now. In any case, he forgot their faces long ago.

## 2.

She was a petite, large-eyed, sulky-mouthed girl from the Mediterranean city of Antakya in southern Turkey, and no matter what she did, people always thought that she was younger than her age. When she turned sixteen, she set her mind on studying abroad. With this obsession, she finished high school, and with this obsession, she slaved and toiled, and succeeded in the end. She found herself in the capital city of a country that in her dreams had taken on legendary proportions, a city that appeared insurmountable with its broad boulevards and maze-like streets. With a meager scholarship she managed to scrape by, and in her free time she took photos and wrote stories which she sold to a news agency for pocket money. She learned the language in one fell swoop, like someone dying of thirst guzzles down a pitcher of water. Let people say what they will, she liked the country and its people. Justice, equality, fellowship, those were the things that mattered to her. It took just a year for her to become more royal than the king and

to start complaining about her own people, who upset and embarrassed her. One day the news agency called. They wanted her to go to
a neighborhood on the north side of the city. They didn't know what
had happened; they only knew that the occupants of a large apartment
building had complained to the police about a Turkish family. They
gave her the address; she got on the metro and went. The notes in
her notebook, before she reported to the news agency, read as follows:
"The Turkish family has lived here for a few months. One man, his
two wives, two grown sons, three young daughters. They live on the
sixth floor, in one of the servant's rooms. At the break of dawn, they
strung up a ram from a tree in the courtyard. The man and his sons
recited prayers, and then cut its throat. The goat is hanging head-down
from the tree. Blood is gushing in the courtyard. A few women have
fainted. Children are crying. People are shouting from their windows.
The Turks cannot explain the situation. They shout that it is the holy
Day of Sacrifice, but no one understands. The police arrest the Turkish
father; his two sons then attacked the police, and were arrested too."

## 3.

He set his coffee on the table and sat down, and squeezing his travel
bag between his knees, glanced anxiously about. He was pale and had
darting eyes, and his large head sat perched upon his tall, thin body as
though it belonged to someone else. For weeks he had been traveling
alone from country to country in Europe. Because he was trilingual,
single, and didn't know how to say no to anyone, he was always loaded
up with the work that others refused to do. He hadn't spoken his
native language for quite a while. That's why, when he heard two men
speaking Turkish behind him, his spirits suddenly rose. Maybe they

would get on the same train. Maybe he would listen to some bits of news that normally wouldn't interest him, but at least would be in his own language. Maybe he would reel off a summary of his travels. Just as he was about to turn, he stopped short when he heard what they were talking about. "This woman was built, I'm telling you. And dressed nice. Actually, I wouldn't say dressed, more like undressed." "Who cares what she was wearing. Did you bang her?" "I'm getting to that. Her flat was on the second floor of an apartment building. It was a real slick joint. We rushed up the stairs, like we were racing. She stopped before opening the door and kissed me. But I was already so horny, I was on fire!" "Enough already, get to the point!" "So anyways, we went inside. But when we stepped in, I froze." "What do you mean, froze? The woman took you to her place, gave you the invitation at the door…" "The house was weird. Everything was black. It was like there was no furniture. Black floorboards, black curtains on the windows, strange pictures on the walls…" "So what? Cut to the chase, you idiot!" "Wait, it isn't over." "Of course not. You had work to do!" "There was nothing to be done, man, it's not like you think." "The bitch was in heat, what else is there to know?" "Then all of a sudden she brought out some handcuffs, a big whip, and ropes and stuff. Like a magician or something. Then she put me in a neck grip, and I was on the ground. Pinned down." "Get out, man, run! That's just messed up!" "I did, I ran for my life. I escaped, and even after downing three bottles of beer, look—my hands are still shaking."

## 4.

She was a lithe girl who sneezed nonstop and her eyes were always watery because of her allergies, and since she didn't know what to do with her stringy blond hair, she cut it like a boy. She could have stayed at the dorm or shared a room with the Turkish girls from school, she could have improved her language skills by working as a nanny for a family, but they didn't let her. Her father had shouted at her that unless she stayed with a relative, she wouldn't be allowed to study abroad. She was put up in the smallest room of the house. But she still hadn't figured out how she was related to this handlebar-mustached relative of hers. He had been married to the same woman for twenty or twenty-five years. The wife was plump, authoritarian and loved to cook, and whether in the bathroom, in the hall, at the kitchen counter, or on the metro or city bus, she always had her nose in a book. This was a woman who despised Turks and had renamed her husband so people wouldn't know he was Turkish. This was a woman who boasted that her family had lived in the same neighborhood for hundreds of years and who, even though she hated change, claimed that she was a revolutionary. The husband and wife didn't get on well together, but they managed. When she left that morning, the wife said that she was going to cook artichokes in the evening. She was always complaining about what a chore it was to carry sacks of groceries up to the sixth floor. So before the wife came home that day, the girl ran to the market and bought six artichokes. She peeled off the leaves carefully. And just as she had learned from her mother, she soaked the hearts in water mixed with flour and lemon juice. Then, heaping peas and carrots on the hearts and adding some olive oil, she put them in the refrigerator. When the wife came home from work, the girl announced her accomplishment: "I cooked artichokes, so you don't need to bother." "Where are they?" the wife asked. "In the refrigerator," she said. The wife opened the refrigerator. "They aren't here." "There, on the glass plate." The wife took out the plate and examined it carefully. "These?" "Yes," the girl

answered triumphantly. "I asked you where the original artichokes are."
The wife was puzzled. "You're holding them." "Tell me how you made
these." The girl explained. Without waiting to hear the end of the explanation, the woman dove for the garbage, scooped out the leaves, and
began spreading them on the table. "The artichokes are in the garbage!
What do you know about artichokes!" That day, the girl learned that in
this country, they boil the leaves, dip them in sauce and nibble the meat
off the tips of the leaves, and throw the hearts into the garbage.

## 5.

He could have been Woody Allen's brother. He looked like him,
just a little bigger, but not the least bit funny; in fact, he was always
quite serious. His ambition had been to work for the World Health
Organization, but after sending abroad quite a few applications and
receiving a positive reply from a prestigious hospital, he didn't hesitate.
He was fed up with being ill-treated at the local government hospitals.
He packed his bags and left. While trying to acclimatize to life in the
new city and to the rules of the hospital, he found out that there was a
well-respected Turkish professor in another department. The professor
had worked there for nearly twenty years and had secured a good
position. A bit shyly, he knocked on the professor's door. The professor
was quite cordial with his upstart colleague. He even invited the young
doctor to dinner at his house on the weekend. That day the snow was
blowing down. He bundled up, brought along his city map, and after
changing buses three times, he trundled through the snowy streets
of the neighborhood and finally arrived at a rather pleasant-looking
house with a large yard. The professor lived with an Italian woman.
Of course, he didn't ask if they were married. They had just risen from

the dining table, which had been heaped with Italian delicacies, when someone knocked on the door. The snowstorm was raging outside. As soon as the Italian lady of the house opened the door, she called out for the professor, fright in her voice. Our character, unable to restrain his curiosity, fell in behind them. At the door there was a man, the left side of his face wounded, and not just his head but his entire body was spattered in blood. Just a few steps away he had been hit by a car. The car that hit him had driven off. The man's cell phone was broken. He wanted to tell his family about what happened and call an ambulance. The professor and the Italian woman whispered to each other and decided to bring the wireless phone to the door. The man was standing in the yard, and he shivered in the flurrying snow as he called home and summoned an ambulance. He thanked them and began limping towards the sidewalk. As the professor and the Italian woman were closing the door, our character snatched up his coat and called out behind the man. "Wait! I'm coming with you." They stumbled into the blizzard and disappeared. He never met with the professor again.

# Journey

Müge İplikçi

*Translated by* ***Mark David Wyers***

They hugged. They were both social people.

They had chanced to meet in the airport of a foreign country, with its certain standards. Germany. Berlin's Tegel Airport.

For a while they chatted, asking what they had been doing and how everything was going. They hadn't seen each other for twenty years.

Up to that point, everything was fine. Children, spouses, work, job successes… After that, there was nothing to talk about, no mundane remarks to label the moment.

Then it was time to wait. The luggage. For some reason, they wanted to wait standing side by side. Standing there, saying nothing.

Both of their eyes were on that opening from which would tumble those small rectangular loads. In the woman's suitcase there were books, and in the man's suitcase were the dress shirts he would wear to the conference in Berlin, and matching ties.

In the woman's: toothbrush, shampoo, hair dryer, and even a slice of cake.

In the man's: professional magazines, electric shaver.

The woman never went on journeys without a mirror and makeup, she never forgot to bring the foundation that concealed her pallor, or the transparent powder, the eyelid cream. She was all care and radiance. And, there was the suede shoe polish, to keep her new shoes radiant.

The man had long been on a diet. Ever since he was diagnosed with high blood pressure, he had learned to control what he ate. In his suitcase, blood pressure medication and vitamins. Being healthy, or at least appearing healthy: at middle age, the primary pursuit. Like they said, to age gracefully. Youth had passed long ago. Their sentences were more mature now; they had exclamation marks, semicolons, commas.

If you look more deeply into their leather luggage: in the woman's, a scarf of intense red and her spirit that challenges the progression of years; in the man's, the philosophy to which he had set his mind at one point, to quickly acquire everything.

That's how they stood, looking at the horizon. The horizon of luggage. But a rift opened in this skyline, for both of them. Nearly at the same moment. Together, they saw an April evening of twenty years before. Hagia Sophia was clearly visible on the other shore. They sat on a bench, on the back of the bench. There were irises in the young man's hands. The purple and yellow flowers were a gift from the girl for his nineteenth birthday. Happiness was in the girl's hands. She was shaping it with her fingers, and the young man spoke of the film they had just seen, and of the strange surprises in life. The film was a journey. The journey of a middle-aged man and woman into the unknown. In the film, the man wandering the winding paths of life was a politician; the woman, a ceramicist. They had come together by chance. The girl will turn to the young man and say, "There was no way they could ever be together." As for the young man, he would gaze at the ancient light reflected in her face from the historical peninsula of Istanbul and brush his lips against her dark curls of hair. His voice would mature with that touch. His breath grazed the girl's happiness.

The luggage began to arrive slowly. Then more quickly. The peninsula was shattered and stones resembling suitcases began to rain down upon them in the waiting area of the airport. One of them was the suitcase of the politician in the film: new, black, awkward, large. Another of them was the woman's: earth tones, sturdy. Then, another suitcase: inside, the words that the politician said to the ceramicist in the final scene of the film: "I am lost in your world, I can't breathe there; this truly frightens me." After that, another suitcase arrives, blue-green. This was the Istanbul of the historical peninsula that appeared and disappeared in the fog.

Then came the woman's brown suitcase, a reflection of herself. She reached for it, her hair straight and short. It appeared that everything was very clear. At least for the woman. Her past had long been hidden away in narrow airless spaces, long been suffocated in sacks. But still, the question "why" kept repeating in her mind. She was angry that her past, with its mistakes and good deeds, had been stolen from her. The man had left her, without a glance back. And the woman? Could her condition be called an obsession with the past? Or just foolish? Spoiled? Childish? If only she could have stayed that way... She had grown up and her spirit was old and weary.

She pulled on the handle of the suitcase, releasing the metal extension. She could go now. But something held her back.

The woman observed the memories in the man's eyes that had long been ignored. She saw a thick sadness in those eyes that used to gaze at her. In the childish arc of those eyes, she saw not that old enthusiasm, but rather a bitterness.

"What's wrong?" she wanted to ask, but her throat stuck.

There was an air of resignation about the man. In his mind, life was the power that drove the carousel that carried the suitcase; for the woman, it meant being a suitcase, moving along on the most well-ordered carousel.

In the end, Yonca asked, "How is everything going?"

Hüseyin answered, "Generally, everything is fine." Implying that no longer did anything special emerge on the shores of his life.


A plane arrived from Italy. A fresh sense of exhaustion filled the waiting area.

Life consisted of journeys. Both of them had learned this over time, sometimes from moments that could be considered strange, sometimes from moments that were unremarkable. At such a juncture, it would be best if any words tinged with romanticism just slipped by, words that were forgotten in the past, in dreams, perhaps on the airport tarmac.

"If generally everything is fine, that's good," Yonca said.

"Yes, in any case, health is the most important thing."

Their pose was like one from an old photograph. Glances from a bench on the shores of the Bosphorus. The waters of the Bosphorus perfectly still. The sudden cessation of conversations and jokes about a shared future. A state of being lovestruck in which the future held no importance at all, as the unknown moved towards them as they approached their twenties, a future that had perhaps not yet been created. In any case, this was the place to which they would arrive. An interval of twenty years. Berlin. Two strangers. Different relationships, losses, solitudes.

Then Hüseyin's black suitcase arrived. Everyone was responsible for their own luggage, that's all. A slightly intimate hug. That's all.

"See you, Hüseyin."

"See you, Yonca. Take care of yourself."

Was that it? In Yonca's suitcase, an uncanny fogged remnant of the past in the way that Hüseyin said "Take care of yourself" that she would obsess over, and then it would vanish; in Hüseyin's suitcase, perhaps regret, but maybe it could be said that it was something stranger than regret. Yonca, reeling from the shock of coming face to face with the past like this, pulled her suitcase, or maybe it was pulling her, and she suddenly found herself in front of an elevator that was sequestered in an odd corner of Tegel airport. It would be enough if she could just get out. A pain throbbed behind her eyes, the kind that would find relief when it mixed with her tears.

The elevator door opened as if into the unknown, and she took shelter inside, but what was the use? Just as the doors were closing, a hand reached in.

"Hüseyin," she thought, and her heart thumped.

He might say, "Yonca, I forgot to tell you something." Or:

"Where are you staying in Berlin?"

"Yonca…"

"Yonca, do you remember?"

Could she say:

"I don't know"?

"Love doesn't bear life onwards"?

"Let's meet at the Berlin Wall, where it was torn down the most"?

"Growing up is explosive"?

"All walls are actually earthen"?

"Meet me at the Brandenberg Gate"?

"A door only opens once"?

But it was far too late at that point to say those things.

It was neither youth nor Hüseyin that had come. It was one of the

Italians from the waiting area. In stilted English, he asked which floor. She said the fifth, as if there were one. The doors of the elevator closed sluggishly.

"Elevator is very slow," the man said.

"So long as we don't get stuck in here," Yonca said.

"You women," he said with a distant friendliness, "you all afraid to be stuck in elevators."

"Everyone is claustrophobic," Yonca said, "even men, but you just don't show it."

"No," he replied, "no, no, no." It seemed as though he wanted to say something more, but couldn't find the words.

If it had been a different time, Yonca would have replied to this bizarre obstinacy with a mischievous smile, slapping him with a "Mammammia!" But she couldn't say anything in any language. She lowered her head in silence. All of the words in the world had stopped there and paused. Her eyes drifted to her suitcase, which reached halfway up her waist and seemed to have become one with her body; she let one teardrop fall, upon its surface.

# While Waiting for the Train

Ayşe Kilimci

*Translated by Sema Yazgan and Mark David Wyers*

Are you waiting for the train, *hanım*?

How'd you know I was Turkish?

I could tell by the way you draped the yarn around your neck and your five-point knitting.

Just killing time, not 'cause I need socks.

How nice. Are you going to sell them?

If you'd like… I could sell them to you cheap.

I'd like that. They have the colors of my hometown, and a hyacinth pattern that's the same in the village where I grew up.

But the hyacinth is the same everywhere in the world.

You've finished one, and you can knit the other while we wait for the train. The heel is already done. How much for the pair?

There's no need to pay. You recognized the hyacinth. Just have them and give your blessings.

No, that would never do. I'll pay up front, the German way.

Just look at you women chatting, I've missed Turkish so much! It's so lovely, the two of you sitting there, talking in the mother tongue.

Let me give you a hug and a kiss on the cheek. How wonderful, three compatriots in a foreign land, three kin… The world is so small, and look, the hyacinth is the same too.

Sometimes the world is small, but at times it's too big, you'd be surprised. Suddenly you find that a loved one is a few countries away.

You're talking about that feeling of missing someone…

Dear girl, people find themselves burning with longing in places like Berlin because of rash decisions.

Maybe that's just how it is.

Like when there is an impassable mountain between you and the one you miss.

No matter how high a mountain may be, there is always a path over it.

What a blessed thing to say. How does the rest of it go?

However bold a man may be, a slave is he to his beloved.

Words are such powerful things, they can hurt and they can heal. If you don't mind me asking, where are you from in the motherland?

Kırıkkale.

From the town?

No, a little outside town. Not exactly outside actually, three or five kilometers away. A place called Yahşihan. And you?

I don't even know anymore. I lived in the neighborhood of Balat in Istanbul for a long time, but I ended up here years and years ago.

I didn't just show up here or anything, I came with my pride and honor from Yahşihan. My folk had never even been to the provincial town, but I crossed the border and now here I am, a native of Berlin.

Now just look at the way those infidels are staring at us. We've got to stick together.

Let them look, I belong here as much as they do. I know the old station in this Berlin of ours, and the new one too. Call them infidels, but I have a past here, and friendships too.

I was in this other place for a long time, in Marzel.

Where's that?

My mother calls it Marsilya, but these Avropeans call it Marseille, just like they say "Pari" when it has always been "Paris."

And this is our Berlin, the capital of Germany.

I know that, of course.

Back home I had never even been to the town center in Kırıkkale, it may as well have been on another planet.

I know Berlin well. This glass hall is part of the largest station in the world, and it has those six glass ervalators...

It isn't "ervalator", it's elevator.

My nana used to call those lifts that my grandpa fixed "ervalators".

Was his name Erva by any chance?

Why yes, how did you know?

Let me tell you, ladies, ever since I came to Europe, my mind has opened up, that's why I know so much. Thanks to Allah, I have my own ideas and opinions.

A woman has to be smart.

Don't call that Berlin Hauptbahnof just a station. With its seven floors you would think it's an apartment building. Just think how about many *avro* our government forked over for it, a fortune!

*Maşallah*, may Allah protect our country and people.

This isn't our country, this is Alamanya! Here, they don't even know that Maşallah means "blessed by God".

But we're one of them now, aren't we? Isn't it kind of ours now too?

Our station was so small, all those years ago...

The one in Yahşihan?

There wasn't a station in Yahşihan, it was just a stop. I am talking about the Berlin Hauptbahnof.

Well, you just said "our" station. Anyways, I am fond of our train stations back at home... So lovely! Just a single story, the building painted yellow, flowers blooming.

We used to have a neighbor who worked at the station as a dispatcher, may Allah bless him if he is still alive, and if he's passed away, peace be upon him. His name was Rıza Beyamca. He was like an uncle to us. The government put up some lines of poetry in the station, and he wrote them down and gave them to me. I've read them a lot since coming here. They're here in my waist pocket, in my small purse... Now where are they? Ah, here they are, the paper's a bit wrinkled but you can still read them, I'll have to put on my glasses. "Trains were our toys, like puzzles in our hands... What beauteous days of play, those long days of longing."

So you think homesickness is some kind of toy then? Hand me my kerchief from that other pocket.

From this station of ours, trains leave every three minutes for other countries. What are you tinkering with there?

Point lace.

It always seems that we're drifting through the world like rootless flowers...

Is that what we are doing?

Well sure, since our people came from Central Asia.

Galloping on horseback...

The children in baskets, the women on the rumps of the horses...

No, that's not how it was. Our ancestors came on horses and camels with their glorious tents, but over years, many journeys, it wasn't easy.

Women would pin their knitting needles in the folds of their skirts, and battle the world with swords.

Surely, that's how it must have been. Maşallah, you know so much.

God willing, my son will open a *lahmacun* shop in our neighborhood. He's thinking of naming the shop "Maşallah" if he gets the permit.

What if he doesn't?

Hopefully he will. People will think "Maşallah" is a huge company, because you see it on all the bumpers and mud-flaps of the buses and trucks that Turks drive.

Just look at this, they built the biggest station in the world right next to our neighborhood. But after it was built, rents went up. Still, it's easy to get around now. I hope we'll stay here for years to come. I come here to the station like I used to go to the park back home, to see something more of the world. It makes me think of the station back in Yahşihan, so humble...

Don't say that, I like the old stations back home, they are so full of cheer.

My mother, who passed away, loved the station building. She used to say it was the apple of the town's eye. The bazaars set up nearby, the people sitting at the cafes watching the trains go by, the station chief swaggering around like a Padishah in his hat and uniform...

She was right. Wherever the railway is, that's where the government goes, where everything goes.

How nice it would be if there were a lahmacun stand around here, we could have a nice snack and chat. Dough rolled flat and baked to a crisp, topped with minced meat and fresh parsley. Your son should open that "Masallah" stand soon, we'll eat there.

Look, here we are at the biggest station in the world and there isn't a single lahmacun shop.

Well, that's how it goes. Every single thing of beauty has a flaw, something missing.

There may not be any lahmacun here, but I have something in my bag.

What have you got?

Dolma.

You don't say.

Praise be to God!

When you eat, ladies, keep it hidden in a napkin, don't let those infidels see it.

It's like living in another world.

That's how it is, my dear. These are different times, and we are different women.

But we're still hardworking and honorable.

The old days flash before my eyes…

You know, in England of this Europe of ours there's a station that has the longest champagne bar in the world.

What's champagne?

It's a sweet drink, like the *sherbet* fruit juice we make back home, but it makes you dizzy, a little like grape juice that's been fermented a bit.

Oh, that bubbly stuff that pops and foams when you open it?

That's it. Not that I have tried it, but once my naughty grandson mixed it with juice and gave it to me one Christmas, and ruined all my prayers.

They weren't ruined.

Pray again, you can make up for them.

And, there's a huge stone sculpture above that station of a man and woman kissing.

This dolma is amazing, God bless the hands that made them. You put in currants, that's not how I do it.

We put in a lot of onions in our dolma, loads of onions.

Probably that's how your people make it, so you do it the same way.

That's the way the women in my home make it, two kilos of sautéed onion for one bowl of stuffing. They also boil the onions.

I chop them as thin as eyelashes and fry them up in olive oil.

In our village we boil them in water, you should do that too. Boil a lot of onions in their own juice.

There are forty restaurants in this station.

Not forty, there are fifteen, and there are cafes too.

So what if there are, there isn't even one lahmacun stand.

Did you know, the Lehrter Bahnhof was first built in 1871. Then it was closed when Germany split up. They tore it down in 1959, I guess, razed it to the ground. After the two Germanys came back together, they rebuilt it as the central station, and a few years after that it was reopened again in May, like an offering for the spring festival of Hidrellez. Escalators, elevators, the whole bit. There are waiting areas, restaurants and coffee shops and TVs, they've got something for everyone. Shops of all kinds, bookstores, shops for clothes from the cheapest to the priciest, and they're open seven days a week.

I hope to God that the lovely old station in Yahşihan is still standing, that it hasn't been torn down. The laws in Germany about opening and closing hours are so strict, but there in Yahşihan the station shops and the bazaar were always open, even when it wasn't market day.

It was like a new wonder of the world, you should have seen how people came to see our station here. They came in heaps. Aren't the seven wonders of the world the "old wonders" that were built before Jesus' time? The Pyramids of Giza, the Hanging Gardens of Babylon, the sculpture of Zeus in Olympus, the Temple of Artemis in Ephesus, the Mausoleum at Halicarnassus in Bodrum, The Colossus of Rhodes, the Lighthouse of Alexandria.

Dear woman, how do you know all that!

My name is Ahçik. I learned about them while helping my grand-children study.

Are you Armenian?

I am, but I am from the motherland. Did you know that my name comes up in folk songs?

No, I didn't.

Haven't you ever heard the song "Bağçalarda Mor Meni"?

Of course, how couldn't I, "Violet in the Garden".

Sing it, if you know it…

"Violet in the garden, I am ill in my heart. Never will it heal, if they keep us apart."

That's not how it goes.

Sing with heart, ladies.

This is our Germany, we are free here…

At one time back home, I mean in Anatolia, the government tried to make us stop singing those old folk songs.

"Violet in the garden, my heart is bleeding through. Ahçik, become Muslim for me, or I'll turn Armenian for you."

My, I've never heard it that way.

When you said you put so much onion in dolma I wondered where you might be from. Don't worry though, we're all one people, and es-pecially in such strange lands we're even closer. It would be rude any-way, no one's better than another, we are all from Adam and the bosom of Islam.

Well, we aren't Muslim.

That's how your people were before Islam came to Anatolia. But now, even though you're not Muslim, you're a migrant. Maybe now's the time to convert? Look how those nice girls and boys hold each other as they walk. If they were back in the homeland, they would have been shot... My grandson says that of those wonders of the world, only the Khufu still exists.

Is Khufu a mummy? The Egyptian who married his sister?

No, it's a stone pyramid in Egypt where the mummies were buried, the one that tourists take pictures of.

Isn't that the one that has the mummy's grave that'll curse you if you touch it? I thought Khufu was the name of the man.

Only parts of the Temple of Artemis remain and they are in the British Museum, and parts of the sculpture of Zeus are in the Louvre Museum. The rest is gone, lost forever.

So there are no more wonders, no eighth, ninth or tenth wonders? You know there are so many back home that if you counted those, the number'd go up to eighteen.

I think that we are the wonders... Nothing could replace us, it doesn't matter what happens to those seven.

You are such a smart woman! Look, I'm adding some embroidery to the socks.

Later, the Eiffel Tower in Paris and the Empire State Building in New York became famous as the new wonders of the world...

Maşallah, you can say words in English so well! I have been living here for years and I still haven't learned German. I draw pictures to get my point across. But of course I only go from home to the restaurant and then back home.

Is the restaurant yours?

No, it's our relatives' Turkish diner, I just work there as a dishwasher.

Do you really think the three of us are wonders?

Sure we are. But we can say that the Berlin Station is one of the wonders too, can't we?

You should've seen it on the opening night, Berlin was lit up with fireworks. The inside of the building is as light as outside because of the glass roof which lets in the sunshine. Each floor is like a balcony because from there you can see the other floors of the building, and at the same time you can see the trains because of the glass. The architect planned the roof to be higher than this. But there wasn't enough money, so the architect was upset.

He was right to be upset.

The trains are so fast! It would be great to take such a trip, I wonder what it's like...

The Hauptbahnhof is even nicer...

We used to say that when you have an Arab horse, everywhere is near and the way is over the mountains. But these days people make the roads go through the mountains. Look, here is the proof.

It's not everyone's destiny to pick up and move to a new place.

That's right.

But moving is also about loss...

What have you lost?

It is nothing, my dear. But... I lost my husband.

You could remarry.

Suffering from one was enough for me. But you know what I mean, a second would only be good for those long nights...

As they say, dawn arrives with or without the crowing of the cock.

If only you'd brewed something up, brought him back.

Why bother when he's the one who left? Good riddance.

Sometimes I wonder if we'd be happier if we hadn't come here.

It's definitely not a pleasant thing, they tear you up by the roots and pack you off.

Like a desperate vine, we clutch the earth, a wall...

You've never wondered if this was the right thing to do?

*Vallah*, never! I'll tell you what, the wishing tree never grows. Forget all that thinking about what could've been.

How'd you come here?

With my husband. But don't ask me how much German I've learned in the past twenty years, I couldn't get anything into my thick head.

When would you have time anyways? Working as a dishwasher, you just go from home to the restaurant and back.

I don't know if that's why, or if it's because life is hard. Back home, my daughter ran off and got married. But the groom was a useless lout, always drunk and chasing other women, and in the end she couldn't take it.

It's tough. We couldn't find a place for ourselves there either.

In that whole big country, we couldn't find anywhere to settle. In the mountains and towns, the bandits and terrorists… We came the illegal way and suffered because of it.

You should have done the paperwork, why did you do it like that?

For a long time we drifted from country to country, and then we snuck across on a train. Now, thank God, here we can go to any doctor we want, but back home it was tough just to get to the village clinic. But you only ask about my sorrow…

Do you remember? When they were having that celebration called Millennium on the English harbor, a bunch of Chinese people were found dead in a truck that had passed through Marche with a load of tomatoes headed for London. You should feel lucky that you are alive, sneaking over the border on a train like that.

Sure we do.

I felt so sorry for them, there were four women and fifty men, and they made it all the way there, but after holding out for so long, they suffocated to death. The tomatoes in the closed container on that truck were still alive but the people were dead. I think they didn't make any noise for fear of getting caught. If only they had kicked and banged so someone would notice.

And it was so hot that year, even back home it was over thirty degrees, it was hell…

Ah, the homeland… What happened to your daughter?

She got divorced and came here to live with us. We were so scared… Sooner or later she was going to move in with us, but we just couldn't get it sorted out, and anyways she'd left school to run off and get married. We were afraid because she was a divorcee, no matter what she did people might think she was flirting, especially in a country like this. You know how people are.

Do you have any kids? Before your husband ran off, at least he could have left a child in your arms.

No, we never had kids. So what happened to your daughter after that?

She married a Pakistani, a university professor. He's dark and a bit lacking in looks, but he treats my blond girl like a queen.

Even if we couldn't be happy back home, at least the children have found happiness in Europe.

That's how it always is. Ours must have been the first.

You mean the ones who make dolma with a lot of onion?

Yes… My mother used to let the children run the streets like scouts. The same as how the dove of Noah brought back the olive leaf. Kids pick up the language so easily, they are the masters of the streets, they play. They make friends with the children of the families here, visit their homes.

Everything is so easy for them, but adults act like such strangers.

That may be true, but look, why are you saying "our" Berlin?

They had an outing one time on a steam train, in memory of the Jewish children who were killed in the world war.

Yes, I remember it like yesterday, people cried a lot.

I went to the exhibition, touched the letters and the pictures. That was the same train company that took all the Jews to the concentration camps, it's like they were trying to pay back a debt.

But they didn't use this new station. The steam train went to the main station in south Berlin and stopped there.

I think they can't face the past, but at least they tried to do something.

Yes, at least they did that. Have you cooked dinner yet?

Today is my off day, and anyways I don't want to cook, my whole life is about doing dishes. We'll just wrap some cheese in pita bread, that'll be enough.

Don't forget the white tablecloth.

And some flowers as well?

That would be fancy.

While waiting for my husband…

Look how we've bloomed like flowers while waiting for the train. Did you see this? I embroidered a rose on the cuff of the sock. It's on me, nothing extra.

Roses are on the house.

Originally it goes, "The tea is on the house."

Where we are from, we say, "Roses are on the house."

Why don't we meet here on our free days, watch the trains, sit in the station park, talk about home. See how nice this is? We've done away with the "if only's", let go of our sorrow and longing, and seen what a world there is out there.

As the saying goes, bees and snakes suck nectar from the same flower, but one turns it into poison while the other turns it into honey.

We'll look out onto this country of ours.

Maybe your son will open his "Maşallah" stand.

So let's come here every week, just like today, to this station made of glass.

God willing, let's do it.

We'll wait for the trains, and talk.

Yes, we'll talk, in Turkish…

# Biographies of Authors

**Semra Aktunç** graduated from the Department of Philosophy, Istanbul University, and then worked as a philosophy teacher at Çamlıca Girl's School. She has published two short story collections, *Başkalarının Fotoğrafı* and *Öyküler Unutmaz*, and has won two short story awards.

**Erendiz Atasü** was born in Ankara in 1947. She graduated from the Faculty of Pharmacy, Ankara University in 1968, and was a professor of pharmacognosy in the same institution until her retirement in 1997. Her short stories written with a feminist consciousness have been published in literary journals, and her essays and articles on literary topics, women issues, secular society and Republican reforms have appeared in journals and dailies. She has published five novels, eight short story collections, six collections of essays, and has received many awards. Her short stories have been translated into other languages and have been published in anthologies in the US, Britain, France, Germany, Holland, Switzerland, Italy, Czech Republic and Croatia. Her novel *The Other Side of the Mountain* (*Dağın Öteki Yüzü*) was published by Milet, and her short story "A Brief Sadness" was featured in *Istanbul in Women's Short Stories*, also published by Milet.

**Zeynep Avcı** was born in 1947 in Kütahya. She tudied at Middle East Technical University (METU), Ankara and at the Department of Sociology, Istanbul University. She worked as a journalist for several newspapers, including *Cumhuriyet, Hürriyet* and *Dünya*, and then in the Paris office of TRT Turkish Radio and Television. She has published five books, and her literary translations in French and English have appeared in magazines and journals such as *Milliyet Sanat, Gösteri* and *Varlık*.

**Nurhayat Bezgin** was born in Ankara in 1954. She graduated from the Faculty of Political Science, Ankara University. She worked for the

Central Bank of Turkey in the US and as general manager in Turkey. She then worked for the Financial Action Task Force of the Organisation for Economic Co-operation and Development (OECD). She has published the short story collection *Karanlıkta Kaybolmayan*, and one of her stories is featured in the anthology *Ankara in Women's Short Stories* forthcoming from Milet.

**Feride Çiçekoğlu** studied architecture at METU, Ankara, and obtained her PhD from the University of Pennsylvania. After the 1980 military coup in Turkey, she was a political prisoner until 1984. She owes her first novel *Don't Let Them Shoot the Kite* (*Uçurtmayı Vurmasınlar*) to the stint in prison. Adapted by the author to screen, it won a number of national and international awards, including the Prix du Public Rencontres Internationales (Cannes, 1989). *Journey to Hope*, which she scripted, won the Academy Award for Best Foreign Film (1991). Her novel and short stories have been published in several languages. From 1995 to 1999, she was the editor-in-chief of the quarterly journal *Istanbul*. She has been Course Director for the graduate program in Film and Television Studies at Istanbul Bilgi University since 2005, and in 2007 she published a book on the representation of cities and women in cinema, *Vesikalı Şehir*.

**Gülten Dayıoğlu** was born in Kütahya in 1935. She studied law at Istanbul University, before deciding to become a primary school teacher and obtaining her teaching certificate. She went on to work as a primary school teacher for 15 years. For the last 45 years, she has continuously contributed to children's and young adult's literature. In 2004, the Turkish Ministry of Education named Dayıoğlu the most read author of all time. She has won numerous awards and her stories have been translated into many languages and published in several anthologies.

**Feyza Hepçilingirler** was born in 1948. She graduated from the Istanbul

Teacher Training College and from the Turkish Language and Literature Department, Istanbul University. At present, she is a lecturer at Yıldız Technical University, Istanbul. She has written prolifically and won several awards, including the Success Award in the Turkish Ministry of Culture, Children's Works Competition (1979) for her play *Yanlışlıklar*; the Sait Faik Short Story Award (1985) for *Eski Bir Balerin*; the Balkan Writers' Association Borski Grümen Award (1991) for her short story "Ne Güzel Ölmüştüm"; and the Sedat Simavi Literature Award (1997) for her short story book entitled *Savrulmalar*. Her short stories have been translated into French, German, English, Serbian and Croatian.

**Aysel Özakın Ingham** was born in Urfa in 1942. She studied French language at the Ankara Gazi Education Institute and taught at the Institute and at several high schools. She continued her studies and work in France, then returned to Turkey and was as a lecturer at the Istanbul Atatürk Education Institute and later at the Istanbul State Conservatory. She started writing and translating in 1977. She moved to Germany in 1980, then to England, where she married the British painter and sculptor Bryan Ingham. She has published seven books, including the acclaimed novel *Gurbet Yavrum* (1975), and her work has been translated into English, French, Dutch, German and Greek.

**Müge İplikçi** was born in Istanbul. She graduated from the English Language and Literature Department, Istanbul University, and received MA degrees in women's studies from Istanbul University and The Ohio State University. She made her mark at a young age, winning the prestigious Yaşar Nabi Nayır Young Author Award in 1996. She has since published four short story collections and three novels, as well as two books of non-fiction. İplikci is a member of Writers in Prison Committee of Turkish PEN, and she has been the chairperson of the PEN Turkish Women Writers Committee since 2007. Her short story "A Question" appeared in *Istanbul in Women's Short Stories* published by Milet, and her novel *Mount Kaf* is being published in English by Milet as well.

Karin Karakaşlı was born in Istanbul in 1972. She studied translation and interpreting at Boğaziçi University. Her first book *Ay Denizle Buluşunca* (1997) earned a mention award in the Bu Publications Novel Competition, and she received the Yaşar Nabi Nayır Young Author Award in 1998. Along with her novel, she has published the short story collection *Başka Dillerin Şarkısı* (1999) and the poetry collection *Benim Gönlüm Gümüş* (2009). Her moving short story "An-bul-ist" was featured in *Istanbul in Women's Short Stories* (2012). She was editor, columnist and head of editorial department at the Turkish-Armenian weekly newspaper Agos from 1996 to 2006, and currently writes columns for the newspaper *Radikal 2*. She teaches Armenian at the Getronagan Armenian Lycee in Istanbul and is lecturer at the Department of Translation Studies, Yeditepe University.

Ayşe Kilimci was born in İzmir in 1954. She graduated from the Social Services Academy, Ankara. In her role as a social worker, she has heard the stories of people from many different walks of life, and her experience in this field has contributed to her writing. Mainly an author of short stories, Kilimci also writes essays and children's books. Her first story appeared in *Varlık* when she was 17, and she completed her first book when she was 19. She has 30 books published and has won several international awards for her stories. For Kilimic, writing short stories is a way to resist injustice, cruelty and despair, and to provide shelter.

Zerrin Koç was born in Samsun in 1956, was educated there, and married in 1972. She wrote poems in protest of the 1980 military junta, and her poetry was first published in the *Sanat Olayı* in 1985. She wrote two novels in 1986, then began to write short stories. In 1987, her first short story "Maide" was published in *Varlık*. Since then, her stories and essays have appeared in *Varlık* and other magazines, and she has published four books.

Hatice Meryem was born in 1969 and is an Istanbul-based novelist and short story writer and former editor of the literary magazines *Öküz* and *Hayvan*. Her books include the novel *İnsan Kısım Kısım Yer Damar Damar* (2008) and the surprise bestseller short story collection *Sinek Kadar Kocam Olsun Başımda Bulunsun* (2002).

**Işıl Özgentürk** was born in Gaziantep in 1948. After graduating from the Faculty of Law, Istanbul University, she began writing plays and scripts, including works for children as well as adults. Her children's plays have been performed by Istanbul City Theatres. She wrote the script for the film *Seni Seviyorum Rosa*, which she also directed. She has represented Turley in international films festivals, winning many awards. Over the years, she has conducted interviews for *Cumhuriyet* newspaper and she continues to write for the paper today.

**Tezer Özlü** was born 1943 and died young in 1986. She was one of Turkey's most original writers. Her first work, the short story collection *Eski Bahçe*, was published in magazines. Her novel *Çocukluğun Soğuk Geceleri* is a life story of suffering abuse and rejection because of being different, told in a sensitive and moving way—"feeling it in the flesh", in the author's words. Özlü won the Marburg Prize for Literature (1983) for her narrative in German *Auf den Spuren eines Selbstmords*, a search for the meaning of life that follows the traces of her three favorite authors: Svevo, Kafka and Pavese. She later translated this work into Turkish under the title *Yaşamın Ucuna Yolculuk*.

**Handan Öztürk** is an author and film director. She was born in Tunceli and raised in Istanbul. She graduated from the College of Press and Distribution, Istanbul University, then moved to Sweden, where she worked at Radio Förderband as a program producer and presenter. After studying cinema and directing at the Hamburg Film Institute, she returned to Turkey and made noteworthy documentaries and the feature film *My and Roz's Autumn* (*Benim ve Roz'un Sonbaharı*, 2007). She has also made series, programs and commercials for Turkish and foreign television channels. Her short story "Stripped of My Bikini by Poseidon" was published in *Istanbul in Women's Short Stories*. She spends most of her time traveling to different countries, journeying into new cities, villages and cultures.

**Yıldız Ramazanoğlu** was born in 1958 in Ankara and is a graduate of the Faculty of Pharmacy, Hacettepe University. She has worked with various women's organizations. Her first writing appeared in the weekly newspaper *Genç Arkadaş* under the pseudonym Elif Yıldız. Her short stories are collected in *Derin Siyah* (1998), and her essays in *Bir Dünya Kadınları* (1998).

**Suzan Samancı** was born in 1962 in Diyarbakır. She has published four short story collections, *Eriyip Gidiyor Gece* (1991), *Reçine Kokuyordu Hêlîn* (1993), *Kıraç Dağlar Kar Tuttu* (1996) and *Suskunun Gölgesinde* (2001), and two novels. Her short story "Kıraç Dağlar Kar Tuttu" came second in the Orhan Kemal Short Story Award in 1997. *Reçine Kokuyordu Hêlîn* has been published in German, Flemish, Spanish, Italian and Swedish, and the collection *Kıraç Dağlar Kar Tuttu* in German. Her story entitled "Perili Kent" was published in a Turkish–German bilingual anthology. *Reçine Kokuyordu Hêlîn* was published in Kurdish under the title *Bajare Mırınê*, and *Suskunun Gölgesinde* as *Siya Bêdengiyê*. Many of her individual short stories have been translated into English, Spanish, French, German, Arabic and Sorani. Her story "In the Melancholy of Wisteria" is featured in *Istanbul in Women's Short Stories*. Since 1995, she has been a newspaper columnist, writing for *Demokrasi*, *Gündem* and *Özgür Politika*, and currently for *Taraf*.

**Selma Sancı** was born in 1958. She studied painting and graphic design. She has been an editor for Turkish newspapers and publishers and currently works for a publishing house in Istanbul. In edition to this collection, her short stoires have been published in the anthologies *Kadın Öykülerinde İzmir* and *Kadın Öykülerinde Doğu*. She published her first book of short stories *Espas* in 2012.

**Mine Söğüt** was born in Istanbul in 1968. She studied in the Department of Latin, Istanbul University, completing her BA in 1989 and later her MA. She began her career in journalism in 1990, and worked as a reporter, writer or editor for the newspapers *Güneş Gazetesi* and *Yeni Yüzyıl*, the weekly news magazine *Tempo*, and the monthly magazine *Öküz*. In 1993, she was awarded an honorable mention in the News category of the Turkish Journalists Association competition. She was a screenwriter for the television documentary series *Haberci* from 1996 to 2000. Her writings and interviews have appeared in numerous newspapers and magazines, and she has published four novels, including *Beş Sevim Apartmanı* (2003) and *Kırmızı Zaman* (2004), both of which were translated to other languages, and the short story collection *Deli Kadın Hikayeleri* (2011). Her powerful story "Why I Killed Myself in Istanbul" was published in *Istanbul in Women's Short Stories*.

**Menekşe Toprak** was born in Kayseri in 1970. She studied political science at Ankara University and worked for a bank in Ankara and Berlin for four years afterwards. She has been working as a radio journalist since 2002, and divides her time between Berlin and Istanbul. Her short stories have appeared in literary journals in Turkey and in Germany, France and Britain. Her published books include the short story collections *Valizdeki Mektup* (2007) and *Hangi Dildedir Aşk* (2009), and a novel *Temmuz Çocukları* (2011). Her story "Transaction" was featured in *Istanbul in Women's Short Stories*.

**Tomris Uyar** (1941–2003) was born in Istanbul and graduated from the Faculty of Economics at the Journalism Institute, Istanbul University in 1963. She was one of the founders of *Papirüs* Literary Review. Her essays and criticism were published in prominent journals like *Yeni Dergi*, *Soyut* and *Varlık*. Uyar is considered one of the masters of Turkish short story writing from the post-1960 period. She published ten story collections, and two of these, *Yürekte Bukağı* (1979) and *Yaza Yolculuk* (1986), won the Sait Faik Short Story Award. She also translated more than 60 books. Her diaries recounting a period of five years in her life were published in five volumes.

**Buket Uzuner** was born in Ankara in 1955. She trained as a biologist and environmental scientist, stuidying and working at universities in Turkey (Hacettepe University and METU), Norway, Finland and the US. She has written numerous short stories, travelogues and novels. Her books have been on the Turkish national bestseller lists since 1992, and have been translated into eight languages. Uzuner won the Yunus Nadi Prize (1993) for her novel *Balık İzlerinin Sesi (The Sound of Fishsteps)*, and her novel *Kumral Ada–Mavi Tuna (Mediterranean Waltz)* was named the Best Novel of 1998 by the University of Istanbul. Her short story collection *A Cup of Turkish Coffee* (2001) was published in dual language Turkish–English by Milet. Uzuner was selected as one of the 75 Most Influential Women of the Republic of Turkey as part of the country's 75th anniversary celebration.

**Yasemin Yazıcı** was born in İzmir in 1957. She worked first as a journalist and writer for the newspapers *Demokrat İzmir* and *Cumhuriyet* and the magazines *Yazko-Somut* and *Sanat Olayı*. She then became a screenwriter and assistant director in the film industry. Her published works include the novels *Kaybolan Kasaba* (1990), *Saklambaç Oynuyorduk Zamanla* (1998) and *Vampir Tangosu* (2004), and the short story collection *Tırtıl Yağmuru* (2008).

# Biographies of Translators

İdil Aydoğan was born in London and grew up in both London and İzmir. She completed her BA in English language and literature at Ege University and received her MA in comparative literature from King's College, London University. Her English translations of Turkish short stories have been published in magazines and books, including nine translations in the collection *Istanbul in Women's Short Stories* published by Milet, for which she was also co-editor.

Alvin Parmar was born in England in 1976. After studying French and Arabic at Cambridge, he spent ten years in Istanbul, where he learned Turkish and got involved in literary translation. He currently has twelve published translations to his name, including three novels published by Milet and two plays that have been performed in New York.

Mark David Wyers was born and raised in Los Angeles, California. He first moved to Turkey in 2001, living in Kayseri and Ankara for several years. He then returned to the US to formally pursue his study of Turkish, supplementing his BA in literature with an MA in Turkish studies at the University of Arizona. He is currently the director of the Writing Center at Kadir Has University, Istanbul. His translations have been published by the literary organization Het Beschrijf, in *Transcript*, and in *Istanbul in Women's Short Stories*. In addition to translating from Turkish and Late Ottoman to English, he is researching Turkey's social history, focusing on gender and marginality. His book titled *"Wicked" Istanbul: The Regulation of Prostitution in the Early Turkish Republic* was published in 2012.

Sema Yazgan has spent most of her life in Istanbul. In 2005, she received a degree in psychology from Istanbul University, and in 2011, she graduated from the Department of American Culture and Literature, Kadir Has University. She does multilingual translations in Turkish, Zazaki, Kurdish and English, and she also works as an English teacher.

Yazgan writes poetry as well as short stories, and her writing has won awards, including an award in Kadir Has University's creative writing competition.